# A Journey through the

# Dark

## THERE'S NOTHING IN THE DARKNESS THAT ISN'T IN THE

# LIGHT

### R.S. Gunn

ISBN 978-1-64559-527-4 (Paperback)
ISBN 978-1-64559-528-1 (Digital)

Covenant Books, Inc.
11661 Hwy 707
Murrells Inlet, SC 29576
www.covenantbooks.com

# PROLOGUE

It was five thirty in the evening. Dawn's pregnancy was taking its toll on her; she was tired, but it was time to start on dinner. Her husband would be home soon, and she had invited her brother over as well. On her way to the kitchen, she paused outside of her daughter Lexie's room. She was three and a half years old and had a wonderful imagination. She would play by herself for hours and never struggle to be entertained. Dawn could hear her talking to her toys and smiled when Lexie let out a heartwarming giggle. Content that her daughter was fine, Dawn continued to the other side of the house and started her meal prep.

As she stirred and spiced each pot, she was usually very content. Cooking was always a peaceful time for her. It was easy for her to get lost in the meal, but something about today was different. In the pit of her stomach, she knew something was wrong. That eerie feeling when something bad is about to happen. Certain that it was just hormones exaggerating her senses she continued on, stopping occasionally to listen for her daughter.

The meal was ready. All Dawn had left to do was let it all simmer so the spices could come to life and do their jobs. One last taste, and she sat the lid back in its place. As she lowered the flame, Lexie came running into the kitchen. Not out of alarm, but at three, it seemed to be the only speed in which she was capable of traveling.

"Hey, sweetie!" Dawn greeted her daughter. "I heard you playing in your room. Who were you talking to?"

"The Blanket Man," Lexie replied as she danced around the kitchen.

"Oooh, the Blanket Man. What did you talk about?" Dawn asked, envying the imagination of her child and expecting a story about unicorns.

"I dunno," was her only reply.

Dawn laughed. "What do you mean you don't know?"

"The Blanket Man comes to my room when I'm playing. He likes to talk," Lexie said, her voice more serious than whimsical.

Dawn stopped smiling. The bad feeling in the pit of her stomach returned with a vengeance. She had been preparing to set the table, but she stopped and turned to her daughter.

"Baby, what does the Blanket Man say?"

"He says that everything he says is the truth and that I should listen to him. He says that there is only his truth," Lexie replied, shaking her head. "But I don't like him."

Now Dawn knelt down to Lexie, the blood drained from her face as the nausea built inside her stomach. "I don't want you talking to the Blanket Man anymore. The things he says are not true. He is not welcome here."

"Okay, Mama," Lexie said and then went skipping out of the room.

Dawn sat down on the floor, trying to calm her stomach and her nerves. The baby was kicking as she did breathing exercises to try and settle him down, but he felt it just as much as she did. They may never relax again. Her daughter had just had a conversation with an evil she had prayed never to encounter again. She searched her mind for memories she had long suppressed; a tear ran down her cheek as it all came flooding back.

She knew what was going to happen next.

# CHAPTER 1

# The Tree

*You look around, See nothing but a tree*
*Leaves, it has none, and of fruit, it is free*
*You're pulled to it, tugged by evil desire*
*As you draw near, it's engrossed in fire*

A lone tree standing on a hill. Lexie looked around. It was a barren wasteland. There were no bushes, no rivers, no animals, and no sound. The only thing she could see was the tree standing in stark black contrast to the blazing white sky above. It hurt too much to look up, but even with all the light, she couldn't see anything else around her. The tree seemed like the only place worth going.

She weighed her very limited options and, hesitantly, decided that it was time to move. She didn't know how she got here or where "here" was, but she knew she had to try to find someone. It came as a surprise to herself that she wasn't afraid. *Maybe it's a dream*, she thought. *Maybe past the tree is Fairyland, and I'll get to dance with unicorns and have dessert with the Fairy Queen.*

She smiled to herself and took the first step; a feat she didn't realize would be quite so momentous. Movement and sound seemed to be concepts with which the world she found herself in was unfamiliar. She was only fourteen, and even though she was a little tall at 110 pounds, she was very thin. However, lifting her leg for that first step felt more like she weighed 800 pounds. Her first footstep came crashing down like a crack of thunder. The sound surrounded her, and she couldn't help but scream from the surprise.

Her scream was even more powerful than her footstep. The sound started a chain reaction like a pebble dropped into a perfectly calm lake; the ripples growing with intensity the further they moved from her. She watched in terror as the echoes of her fear reached the tree.

What she thought were leaves dangling from the branches burst to life as the wave of sound hit them. A dark cloud rose from the tree without making even a vibration in the stagnant air. Leaving only the barren remains of dead branches in its wake. Lexie didn't know what it was, but she knew it was unhappy, and she knew it was headed straight for her.

Without a second thought, she took off running straight for the tree. She knew it offered her little protection, but her only other option was absolute nothing. Each footstep created the same deafening crash of thunder. She ran faster, as fast as her legs could move. The cloud shooting straight up as if the sound of her running actually caused it pain. She didn't know where this place was, but she knew she had to leave. The longer she stayed, the less it felt like a dream, and the more it felt like forever.

Was she trapped? She just needed the tree.

Gasping for air, she collapsed among the roots of her steadfast savior. Finally, the tree. She closed her eyes and tried to calm her breathing. Then a voice inside her head began to speak, *The tree is truth. My truth. Always listen to my truth, and I will protect you. I've been waiting for so long.*

Lexie was terrified. She knew the voice, and she knew the words. How could he have found her? They had moved so many times. Her mother was desperate to save her from this thing. He couldn't know where she was. Slowly, she opened her eyes. What she thought were roots on the ground now held her tight as a mother's embrace, but these weren't her mom's arms.

Looking up, she saw him, the object of her nightmares and her every fear. There were no eyes, but she knew he was looking straight into her soul. His long tentacle-like arms wrapped around her like a snare, trapping her against the base of the tree and making it difficult to breathe.

"Blanket Man," she whispered, and the sound broke his hold on her. The ground began to shake, and the dark cloud circled them.

*I see you.* His voice declared inside her mind.

"But you can't have me," Lexie screamed out loud.

The tree burst into flame, and the dark cloud grew even thicker, choking her and making it hard to see anything beyond the flames. Anything, beyond him. She turned to run, but someone else was standing there. Someone she had never seen before but felt very familiar. He was just a boy, maybe her age, but she knew he was there to save her.

He reached out his hand, and as soon as she grasped it, he leaned in and whispered, "Wake up." The world around her melted away into total darkness. She closed her eyes and started to cry.

When she opened her eyes again, she was lying in bed in her room. The sun was barely up, but the birds were already chirping. "It was a dream," she said to herself, "a bad dream, but still just a dream."

Lexie climbed out of bed and walked to her window. She knew that her grandparents had left her family this house but hated how close it was to the woods. It didn't matter which direction she turned, there were trees everywhere. No neighbors, no skyscrapers, no traffic, and no peace. Just trees and everything that she had grown to fear. She liked being outside, and she loved the sounds of all the animals and the constant smell of flowers, but she knew she could never go past the trees. They formed her permanent cell. Like a prison warden, he was there, watching her. Even if she didn't see him, she could feel him. It had been years since he had made an appearance, but after that dream, she knew she couldn't let her guard down. He was still looking for her. He was still waiting.

"What are you doing up so early?" Lexie turned from the window to see her mother standing at her bedroom door. "I thought I was the only one who couldn't sleep. Are you feeling all right?"

Lexie just walked to her mother and put her arms around her neck and started to cry. Her mom dropped the clothes basket she was holding and wrapped her arms around her daughter.

"What is it, baby?" she asked. "What happened!?"

Lexie just shook her head as her mom led her back to bed. She kissed Lexie's forehead and looked deep into her eyes. Fear. She could see absolute fear on her daughter's face.

"It was just a dream," Lexie said. "I know it was a dream, but *he* was there. Why can't he just leave me alone?"

Dawn managed a small smile. Her daughter had been dealing with these nightmares for years now, but it had been a while since she had one. Was it too much to hope that they were done?

"He isn't here. It was just a dream. You're safe. I know that it's still scary, but you can't let it get to you. Just stay out of the woods, and you will be fine. Besides, we can't start the day off like this. We're building a new fairy circle when your brother wakes up. Now get dressed and come down to the kitchen, I'll get breakfast started."

"Don't you think I'm a little too old to still be building fairy circles?" Lexie asked with a chuckle. "I'm in high school now. I know fairies aren't real."

Dawn let out a laugh. "Be careful what you say, the fairies will hear you! Age isn't a factor, and if nothing else, your brother still loves it. So let's just go ahead and suffer through it for his sake."

Dawn walked to the bedroom door and started to pick up the clothes she had dropped.

"Mom?" Lexie's voice seemed so small behind her.

"Yes, sweetie?" she answered without turning.

"There was someone else there this time. In my dream. There was a boy. He was my size, and he's the one who took me away. I think he's the reason I woke up. I felt like I knew him," Lexie said.

Lexie saw her mother pause. Slowly, she stood up, basket in tow. She turned and Lexie could see that she was too pale; the blood had drained from her face.

"Well, you see? There you go," Dawn said with a smile that didn't quite reach her eyes. "Someone is always there to look out for you."

Downstairs, Dawn started making breakfast. Pancakes with fresh strawberries would perk Lexie up and help her forget about the dream and all of her fears. Bacon for Cain when he woke up. It's all he ever wanted.

As she mixed the batter, Dawn's mind started to wander. She fixated on a moment in time that she rarely allowed herself to go to. The day she lost her son.

Lexie and Isaac were twins. Dawn's body was too weak. She couldn't carry them both. Isaac was lost, and Lexie thrived. She had had a dream shortly after she lost Isaac. In her dream, she sat in her parents' house, the house she now lived in with her two children, and there was a boy on the couch next to her. She looked at him, and she knew he was hers. He had bright blond hair and beautiful green eyes.

"Why did you leave?" Dawn asked the boy in her dream.

"For Lexie," he replied.

"She'll be lost without you! You're part of her!" Dawn practically shouted as the tears started to pour.

"This is the only way I can go where she goes. I will always be with her. I will guide her when no one else can." He stood up and turned to leave.

"What about me? I need you!" Her words filled with the desperation of a mourning mother.

"I am always with you. I will always love you."

With those words, he was gone, and the dream was over.

"Mama?" The word brought her back to the present.

"You're burning the bacon." Cain said as he rubbed his eyes.

Dawn turned around to the stove to see four black charred pieces of what used to be a breakfast meat.

"No!" She quickly turned off the flame and opened a window to let the smoke out. Frantically, she turned on fans and checked the pancakes to make sure they hadn't suffered the same fate. They had.

Lexie walked in to pure chaos as she entered the kitchen.

"What happened?" She asked as she stepped beside her little brother.

"Mom burned everything, and now I think she might be having a full-on panic attack," Cain replied.

Just then, Dawn stopped her mad dash around the kitchen and looked at her two children. They were absolutely beautiful. Lexie had the same dark blond hair that she had when she was young; she wore it in an angled bob with sharp bangs, and her dark brown eyes had always seemed too wise for someone so young. Cain, on the other hand, was the exact opposite. He had very dark hair that he had to keep short. He hated if it touched his ears. His eyes were more like hers, hazel, and seemed to change a little depending on his mood, and there was a constant hint of laughter always there. He had such a happy soul. She couldn't believe he would be ten in a few weeks.

"How about we go to town for breakfast?" Dawn suggested.

"That works for me," Lexie answered with a smile.

"Do they have bacon?" Cain asked.

Dawn just smiled. "Get your shoes on. We have a date with the fairies when we get back."

As they made their way to the car, Dawn noticed the light sweatshirt Lexie had slipped on, and it made her heart sink. There was something familiar about it when she bought it, but she couldn't place it until now. Before they drove off, she turned to her kids and looked them both in the eyes.

"No matter what happens today," she said in a tone that neither of the kids had ever heard her use before, "you are stronger, and you are braver than you could ever possibly imagine. I love you both with all of my heart, and there is nothing in this world, or any other, that you should fear."

Dawn turned her attention back to the car and started down the road toward town. The look of confusion on their faces was warranted; she knew they had no idea what she was talking about, but she also knew that, very soon, they would.

This was a day she had been dreading for years.

# CHAPTER 2

# The Woods: Part 1

*Above the limbs a dark cloud grows*
*It moves toward you like a flock of crows*
*You cry out in fear and leech to your host*
*But it can't protect you from this unholy ghost*

"I brought extra diamonds for the fairies," Cain said. He called any white rock a diamond, something he had done since he was little.

"You know they're not diamonds." Lexie corrected. "I keep telling you they're just pretty rocks."

"It doesn't matter what you call them. To me, they're diamonds, and I know the fairies love them." Cain smiled as he sat two rocks in the middle of the fairy circle that he and his sister had been building.

"This will give the fairies a nice place to dance, and I'm sure they will love your diamonds."

Dawn liked seeing her kids work together like this. Their cousins had shown them how to make the little fairy circles several summers ago, and the kids couldn't get enough of them.

"We need more sticks to make the walls. Lexie, we need more sticks." Cain could be a little bossy.

"Okay, okay, and we need big leaves." Lexie wandered around the clearing beside their house trying to find anything that she could use to build the walls.

"You kids stay here in the open and don't go near the road." Dawn warned her children. "I'm going to go inside and see if your dad called. I figured he would be here by now." With that, she left the kids to their own devices and disappeared into the house.

"Did you find any sticks?" Cain asked his sister.

"There aren't many lying around," she answered.

Cain stood up from the circle where he was arranging the precious stones for the fairies. He still had a few, but he decided to save them for the next circle and slid them into his pocket.

"There are probably lots of sticks in the woods," Cain said as he stared past the trees.

"You know we can't go in there. Cain, promise me you'll never go into the woods!" Lexie said with just a hint of edge in her voice.

"I don't see what the big deal is," Cain answered without promising. "Just because you're scared of trees doesn't mean I shouldn't get to have fun."

"It's not the trees, and I'm not scared of anything. It's the things that live in the trees…" Lexie stared at Cain and watched as he started to move closer to the woods. "Cain. Don't."

*There's nothing to be afraid of. The woods are magic.* Lexie heard the voice in her head, but she knew it wasn't her brother. *Come see where the fairies live. Come see our magic.*

Cain walked slowly forward, entranced.

"Cain!" Lexie screamed as she started to run after him. "Cain! Turn around!"

She reached out her hand and grabbed her brother's arm. As she did, the object of her terror stepped forward. Everything she dreaded was within feet of her. She lost her grip on her brother's arm and fell backward. Frozen by her own shock, she watched, helpless, as Cain passed through the tree line.

Standing directly beside the Blanket Man, Cain turned and faced his sister. "Look, silly, there's nothing here. There's nothing to be scared of."

"Cain, please, he's right beside you!" Lexie pleaded, "Come back!"

Cain stared at her in disbelief. He couldn't see anything.

*Mother to daughter. Sister to brother. I have what I need.* The Blanket Man reached out and laid his hand on Cain, the long spider-like fingers enveloping his shoulder.

Cain quickly looked up and, for the first time, saw the monstrous creature which had haunted his sister's nightmares. The Blanket Man smiled wide, revealing razor-sharp teeth, and then without a flash, without a sound, he and Cain were gone.

Panicked and terrified, Lexie burst into the front door of the house. Her mother and father were standing in the kitchen; he must have arrived shortly after her mom walked inside.

"He's gone!" Lexie screamed as she collapsed onto the floor. Her parents rushed in and Alex, her father, scooped her up.

"What happened? Who's gone? Where is your brother!?" Dawn forced the words out as the horror in her mind began to spin. She rushed out the front door and started screaming for Cain. There was no answer.

"He took him!" Lexie shouted through her sobs. "I told him not to go into the trees. He couldn't see him! Cain couldn't see *him*! He didn't believe me!"

"Who took him?" her father pleaded. "Who?"

"The Blanket Man," Dawn whispered as she walked back to her daughter. The realization driving a stake into her own heart.

"He put his hand on Cain's shoulder, and they disappeared." Lexie's words were pained. "He wanted me, but he took Cain."

Alex looked at Dawn. His worst fears were being realized. Though he had always believed the stories that their daughter told them about the angry fairy, secretly, he hoped it was all just in her mind—the object of too many of Dawn's scary stories and an overactive imagination.

"Look at me," Alex said, standing his daughter up so their eyes met. "Your mother and I are going to go look for your brother. I want you to lock the door behind us, then go to your room and wait. Don't go outside. Don't open the door for anyone except us. No matter what happens. Do not go into the woods. I know it's scary, but we have to try to find him. Keep the phone close, and if we aren't back soon I want you to call 9-1-1. Do you understand?"

Lexie simply nodded her head as her tears continued to pour. Alex kissed her on the head and stood to walk outside.

"Everything is going to be all right," Dawn said reassuringly to her daughter. "Now do what your father said and lock yourself in."

Dawn and Alex disappeared out the door. Lexie shut and locked it behind them and ran to her room. As worried as she was about her brother, she was still terrified for herself. She slammed her door behind her and crawled under her bed. Curled in a ball, she laid there weeping. Soon, she was lost to sleep.

"Lexie?"

She heard the familiar voice and opened her eyes. She was lying on a grassy hill underneath a giant maple tree. It was the middle of the afternoon, and the sun was beating down. Even though its rays were hot, there was a cool breeze that evened everything out and made it pleasant. Lexie sat up and looked around. How had she gotten here? There was something familiar about this hill, but she couldn't place it. It was like a dream she had had at some point; it felt surreal but peaceful—the sounds of the birds, the whoosh of the wind, and smell of freshly cut grass that was carried on it. It felt perfect, but something was off.

"Lexie?"

She spun around. Sitting behind her was the boy from her dream. He was smiling.

"Where am I?" Lexie asked.

"You're in a safe place, a kind of paradise. A place of light. I wanted to talk to you," he replied.

"Who are you?" she asked.

As she looked around, she realized what made this place feel so odd; there were no shadows. Despite the sun being high in the sky, nothing around her cast a shadow.

"My name is Isaac. You know me. You just have to remember." His smile brightened.

"You're...my brother?" Lexie stared at him. She didn't know how it was possible, but she knew that it was true. "Mom has talked about you."

"See? You knew all along." Isaac picked a flower from the ground beside him and handed it to her.

"But why are you here? Why am I here? I need to get back. Mom and Dad are looking for Cain."

Lexie's mind flashed back to everything that had just happened at her house. What if they found him? What if they were locked out of the house, and she wasn't there to let them in? What if Cain was hurt, and she needed to call an ambulance? Her mind reeled.

"They won't find him," Isaac stated flatly as the smile faded from his face.

The comment brought Lexie back to the moment. "What do you mean? They have to!"

"They won't find him because they're looking in the woods, and that's not where he is anymore. You saw it yourself," he said.

"Where did they go? Where did the Blanket Man take him?" Lexie moved closer to her brother.

"They went to a place where normal people aren't supposed to go. To a place where I can't see. The creature you call the Blanket Man took Cain to Fairyland. He misleads and distracts. He would do anything to keep people from seeing the truth. He has done this since his beginning. Years ago, he poisoned the heart of a most powerful being. Whispering his false truths, she listened and accepted him as a servant. He takes children and offers them as tribute, a gift for the one he deceives. He has had many names and many stories." Isaac explained as best he could to his sister.

"Who would the Blanket Man serve? Who is worse than him?" Lexie asked, in shock.

"Good or bad, all fairies answer to the Fairy Queen, and if you want to get him back, that's who we'll have to go see." He reached past his sister and picked up a box from behind the tree and handed it to Lexie.

"What do I have to do?" she asked as she opened the box. Inside, there was a beautiful silver bracelet. It was big and ornate, covered in etched swirls and symbols. "What is this?"

"I need you to come with me. I'm going to get Cain back, but I need your help. When you put that bracelet on"—Isaac said, motioning to the box—"it will be anything that you need it to be. It will protect you and provide for you. It will guide you. Will you come with me to Fairyland? Will you help me save our brother?"

Lexie took the bracelet out of the box and slid it onto her arm. It shrank to fit her perfectly, and the symbols started to glow with a bright blue light. The smile returned to Isaac's face, and he reached out his hand to his sister.

"What do I have to do now?" she asked as she took his hand.

"Just wake up," he whispered. Again, the world melted around her, and she closed her eyes.

When her eyes opened, Lexie was still curled up under her bed.

"It was just another dream," she said aloud as she slid out into the light.

The sun was setting. She must have slept for a few hours.

"Maybe it was all a dream," she said hopefully. "Maybe Mom and Cain are downstairs!"

Lexie ran to her bedroom door and reached for the handle. When she did, she noticed something around her wrist. Pulling her sleeve back, she saw the beautiful bracelet that Isaac had given her in her dream.

"It was real…" she whispered.

In that moment, she knew exactly what she had to do. Opening her bedroom door, she bolted down the stairs. She paused as she reached for the front door lock. What if it was a trick? What if nothing she thought had happened really had? What if everything had been a dream? What if she was running straight into the trap she had been avoiding her entire life?

Slowly, she unlatched the lock and opened the front door. No one was there. With the questions and doubt still mulling on her mind, she rounded the corner of the house. There, standing just outside the tree line, was the boy from her dream. He was real, and he was in the clearing. He couldn't be a trick.

Her faith was restored in an instant, and she ran as fast as she could to meet him. The two smiled at each other for just a moment then, with a deep breath, they crossed the line into the woods that Lexie had feared for so long.

# CHAPTER 3

# Fairyland and the Gate

*Waiting in the darkness pacing through the night*
*The future seems so certain now dreaming of the light*
*I know now what will happen I've seen it in my sleep*
*I know what will happen and that secret I must keep*

"We need to call the police," Alex said to Dawn as they crossed the clearing headed back to the house. Alex was in panic mode. "We need to call everyone we know and get a search party together."

Dawn was nodding, but she wasn't listening. She was lost in her own mind, forming plans and replaying everything that had just happened.

"Do we know anyone with search d—" Alex stopped midsentence. Looking at Dawn, she was frozen in place, staring into the woods. Her face was completely white, and she wasn't making a sound. Alex slowly turned around, following Dawn's gaze, uncertain of what he was going to see.

"Lexie!" he screamed and started running for the trees as fast as he could.

Lexie and Isaac turned at the sound and saw their father running toward them. Lexie raised her hand to tell him to stop and that everything would be okay, but in that moment, Isaac laid his hand on her shoulder, and they were gone.

Alex stopped just short of the trees and stumbled backward. His daughter had just vanished before his eyes. He turned to Dawn who was slowly making her way toward him; her eyes still fixated on the trees beyond.

"Where is she?" he demanded.

Dawn remained silent.

"Where are our children? Why would she go into the woods alone?" Alex's words made their way to Dawn, and she came back to the moment.

"She wasn't," Dawn said blankly.

Like when Cain disappeared, there was no flash, no sound. Though Lexie and Isaac had disappeared from the sight of their parents, it didn't look to Lexie like they had actually gone anywhere. The only difference was that all the colors seemed muted—a dull version of the world she was used to—and there was a deep fog that had settled just above the ground.

She stared at her parents. She could see the panic in their father's eyes. He was screaming something, but she couldn't quite make it out. Her mother was stoic, aside from the tears that were now streaming down her face.

Lexie called out to her father. "Dad! Dad!"

"He can't hear you," Isaac stated. "Mom will explain it to him. Now we need to go."

The reunited brother and sister walked through the fog-covered woods, toward the sound of flowing water, for what seemed to Lexie to be an eternity. Finally, she could see a river.

"Have you ever been here before?" Lexie asked her brother.

"No," he replied, "there's no place for me here."

"Then how do you know where we're supposed to go?" she asked.

"I can feel Cain. He's scared. He doesn't belong here either." Isaac stopped at the edge of the river and stared into the abyss of trees beyond it. Lexie stopped beside him and could tell that something was wrong.

"What is it?" she asked. "What do you see?"

"The river is a bridge. When we cross over, we will be walking out of the light and into darkness. I have never left the light." Isaac looked down and watched the water flowing past.

"I don't like the dark either. Mom always says that we shouldn't be scared. She says that there is nothing in the darkness that isn't in the light." Lexie put her hand on Isaac's shoulder.

He turned and looked her in the eyes, his fear obvious. "She lied."

He didn't know exactly what it was that they would face once they crossed the river, but he knew it would be bad, and he needed Lexie to be as ready as she could be.

"We're running out of time," he said. "We need to cross."

Hand in hand, both children took the first step into the water. With trepidation, they began to cross. The current was very strong. Stronger than Lexie had expected. She tried desperately to hold on to Isaac's hand, but she kept slipping on the rocks below her feet. The river was too deep; soon, it would be over her head.

"You have to hold on, Lexie!" Isaac shouted over the sound of the rushing water. "You can't let go!"

"I'm tryi—" And with that last syllable still on her lips, she went under.

She couldn't feel her brother's hand anymore. She couldn't feel anything but the cold. Every time she tried to open her eyes, she failed. The riverbed was nowhere near her feet, and she wasn't even sure which way she was facing. She needed air; her lungs were starting to burn. She couldn't hold it any longer. The pain was too much. She let out a scream, and every bit of air she had left was lost to the water.

Then all at once, the rushing stopped. The cold was replaced by the feeling of warm sunshine on her face, and instead of the water tearing at her skin, she felt a comforting summer breeze surround her.

Lexie opened her eyes and was shocked by what she saw. She was standing behind her house. It was the middle of the afternoon, and the sun felt better than it ever had before. She looked around for Isaac, but he wasn't there.

Just inside the tree line, there were three people sitting on a couple of logs. On one side, there was a little girl; she was maybe four or five years old and looked familiar, but Lexie couldn't quite place her. Her long dark-blond hair was wavy and tossed carelessly over her shoulders. Next to her was a woman; Lexie thought it was her mom at first, but then, she realized that this was someone else, someone she knew well. Her shoulder-length chocolatey-brown hair curled around her face in a way that Lexie could never forget.

Across from them, sat another woman. She was young and very pretty and had a pleasant smile on her face. Lexie imagined that she always had that smile. It looked natural. She had very long straight blond hair that she wore back in a ponytail, and her light-blue flannel shirt made her bright blue eyes pop even from this distance.

She moved closer to the trees to see if she could hear what they were talking about. She was doing her best to try and keep herself hidden, but that wasn't an easy task. The young woman was saying something, but Lexie couldn't quite make it out. Her voice was too soft.

"What is she saying now?" the dark-haired woman asked the little girl. Her eyes were darting around the woods like she knew the other woman was there, but she couldn't see her.

"She says her name is Shawna. She says she's your sister." The little girl smiled and looked at the woman across from her. "Well, that makes you my aunt!"

"I'm here to guide you," the woman said to the little girl. "I will show which way to go when you think you are lost."

"She says she's here to guide me, Mom. She won't let me get lost." The girl looked up at her mother. "I don't know what she's talking about."

"Dawn, ask her where she comes from. Ask her if she's a friend." The dark-haired woman insisted. Her motherly concern was brimming.

Lexie stood upright in shock. The little girl was her mother, Dawn. This was the past. The woman next to her was Lexie's Nana.

"I am a friend. I come from the light," Shawna said, still smiling, in response.

"Who's that?" Dawn asked, looking directly at Lexie. Lexie froze. She had been spotted, and she had no idea what to do.

"Who?" her mother asked, looking in the direction that Dawn was motioning. "Do you see someone else?"

Dawn kept her eyes locked on Lexie. "There's a girl," she replied. "She's standing right there by that tree. Can't you see her?"

Shawna stood and moved to Lexie. As she rose, everything came to a halt. The wind ceased to move, and Dawn and her mother appeared to be frozen in place.

"You shouldn't be here," she said to Lexie. Even though she was still smiling, Lexie could hear the edge in her voice.

"Where is here? Is that my mom?" Lexie pointed to the little girl whose motionless gaze was still fixed on her.

"It is. This is her time. You must go back. One brother is looking for you, and another is crying for you. Lexie, look at me." Lexie's eyes shifted from her young mother to Shawna. "Wake up."

Lexie gasped for air. Her lungs were still burning. She was soaking wet and could feel the mud beneath her fingers. She opened her eyes and could see that she was lying on the river bank.

"Lexie?" Isaac's voice was distant and panicked.

"I'm okay!" She shouted back. "I'm here!"

Moments later, Isaac was at her side.

"Are you okay? I couldn't find you!"

"I'm okay." Lexie sat up and looked herself over. She was covered in mud, but there weren't any scratches. The bruises would be coming soon, but she was satisfied that she hadn't broken anything.

"If you're okay, then we need to get moving. He has taken Cain into the depths of Fairyland." Isaac stood and offered his hand to Lexie.

"What do you mean, Fairyland? That isn't a real place. It's just a story that Mom tells us. It always makes Cain happy. That's why we build the Fairy Circles, to make Cain happy." Lexie took her brother's hand and stood up.

"Lexie, those aren't just stories. Your Mom tells you about the fairies so that you will be kind and respect them. She knows how cruel they can be when they're upset. She tells you about the good fairies so that you won't hate them, and she tells you about the bad fairies so that you won't mess with them." Isaac stated.

"How would Mom know any of that for real?" Lexie asked, laughing.

"She's been here." It was a simple response, but the truth of it struck her at the core.

Every story her mother had ever told them came flooding through her mind. She talked about Fairyland as if it were a paradise she had actually seen. The joy, as she told the stories, that Lexie had thought was just faked enthusiasm, now rang true as a vivid happy memory.

"Here?" Lexie asked.

Isaac simply nodded in the direction behind her. Lexie turned and couldn't believe her eyes. It was amazing. It was like that scene in The Wizard of Oz when Dorothy steps out into Oz. Everything had been black and white, but at that moment, she was seeing in Technicolor.

She was still in the woods, but the trees were so huge, they had to be ancient. The moss and ferns that covered the ground were the most vivid green she had ever seen. There were flowers everywhere in every color imaginable, and it sounded like every bird was singing the same harmonious melody.

"I've never seen anything like this before. It's beautiful!" Lexie exclaimed.

A warm breeze swept through the trees, causing a swirl of butterflies to fly up from the flowers and surround Lexie. She couldn't help but squeal in delight.

"I thought you said it would be dark here?" Lexie asked through her laughter.

"This is a paradise. Light shines here. But when you go through the gate, there is only darkness."

"Where does the gate lead?" she asked, looking closely at a beautiful butterfly which had landed on her hand.

"It is the entrance to the Queen's Castle. There are several levels, and her throne is in the center of the very last one."

Isaac walked past the trees to the edge of a clearing, staring across it, he continued, "The Queen used to live up here. She ruled in the light. She is the most beautiful creature that has ever existed. She would watch people. She would even send them small gifts just to see their joy—a beautiful sunset, a warm rain on a summer night, anything to make them smile.

"As time passed, she started to grow weary. She continued to watch people, but she stopped seeing the good. She could only see the ugliest parts of human nature. The anger and greed. She convinced herself that humans didn't deserve all of the gifts that they had been given, and as her anger grew, she retreated further and further into the darkness of her castle. To get Cain back, we'll have to go to her."

Lexie stepped beside her brother. "Where is the gate?" she asked.

Isaac smiled at the resolve he saw on his sister's face and pointed directly across the clearing. "There."

Isaac and Lexie walked across the clearing. All of the wonderful noises they heard fell eerily silent as they approached the gate. It stood out in stark contrast to the beautiful world around it. Nature ended at the gate. Standing fifteen feet tall, the gate itself was made out of solid metal. It gleamed in the sunlight. There were words inscribed across the top, but Lexie couldn't read them.

"What does it say?" she asked her brother.

"Hope," he said solemnly, "has no place here." Isaac looked at his sister. He could see the fear in her eyes. "We won't be welcome. That doesn't mean we won't succeed."

Lexie looked up at the gate. "How do we open it?" she asked. "There isn't a knob or anything."

Isaac stepped closer and touched the gate. "It's locked with dark magic. You need to use your key."

"I don't have a key." She practically laughed as she looked at her brother.

"I gave you one." Isaac looked down at Lexie's wrist where the silver bracelet sparkled in the sunshine.

Lexie looked down at the bangle. "You gave me a bracelet."

23

"It is called the Anauz. It will be whatever you need it to be. Place your hand on the gate." Isaac directed his sister as he stepped back. "You have everything you need to make the key work."

Lexie placed her hand on the gate. The metal was hot from the sunshine's constant gaze. Her hand looked so small.

"What makes me so special?" Lexie said under her breath. "What do I have?"

"Faith." Her brother responded.

As if on cue, as the word left Isaac's mouth, the bracelet started to glow a bright and blinding blue. The light surrounded Lexie, and the joy she felt was insurmountable. She laughed hysterically as the glow radiated beyond her and onto the gate. The metal resisted, but only momentarily. The gate slowly and menacingly opened for the children. The wider it opened, the dimmer the light became, until it faded completely and, along with it, Lexie's joy.

Beyond the opening of the gate, there seemed to be nothing. Even the sunlight couldn't seem to pass beyond the threshold.

"What happens when we walk inside?" Lexie asked her brother, her eyes tried to pierce the darkness.

"I have no idea." Isaac stepped beside his sister and took her hand. "No matter what, we stay together."

Lexie nodded, and the two walked slowly through the opening. As they did, the gate came crashing shut behind them. Wherever they were now, they weren't going back.

# CHAPTER 4

# The Queen's Castle: Level 1

*I stand in the valley, I watch the coming flood*
*All around me, waters rise, then I realize, it's their blood*
*On the hills all around me, on the mountains and the stream*
*Oh, Father God, I plea, let this only be a dream*

*You came.* The voice echoed in Lexie's mind. She looked around; Isaac wasn't there. She was standing in a valley next to a roaring river. She looked up and storm clouds were swirling in the sky. Every few seconds, there was a vibrant flash of lightning and a crash of thunder that shook the ground she stood on.

Lexie's gaze fell to the river. The water was rising quickly; any moment it would break free overtake its earthly captor.

*I knew you would come. I've been waiting for so long.* The voice was growing louder in her mind. *When you were a small child, I told you my truth, and you ran from it. But now you have come to embrace it. Always listen to my truth, and I will protect you...I've been waiting for so long.*

Lexie turned. The evil that had haunted her her entire life was standing right beside her. Towering over her. As she stared into his empty face, the fear she had felt since she was a small child rushed over her in a wave of panic.

"Who are you?" she whispered.

*Who am I?* The voice laughed with disdain inside her head. *I'm your best friend. I'm your confidant. Don't you remember the talks we used to have? Oh, how we would laugh as we told each other stories. I'm the Blanket Man.*

"No," Lexie said louder. The Blanket Man stepped back. "I'm not a little girl anymore. Who are you!?"

*I am...truth. I am...magic. I have had so many names. My favorite has always been Blanket Man. You were such a creative child. However, if you're seeking the first name then, Elymas,* he said as lightning flashed across the sky, and a crack of thunder brought Lexie back to her surroundings.

The river had broken past its bonds, and the water around her was rising too quickly. She looked down, and a new wave of terror swept across her.

"Blood...it's blood," she whispered as she looked back to Elymas. "Where is my brother?" Lexie screamed.

Elymas stumbled backward at the sound. A pained smile spread across his face as she heard his voice again in her head. *Listen to my truth, and you will all be free. Follow my path, and I will show you things you have never imagined. There is nothing to be afraid of. Welcome to Fairyland—*

"Lexie!" Isaac screamed.

Lexie spun around to the sound of her brother. She was no longer in the stormy valley but in a dark cavern. The bracelet on her wrist was glowing its brilliant blue, and she could see her brother running toward her.

"Where were you?" Isaac asked. "When the door shut behind us, you disappeared."

"I was next to a river. It was storming. It was dark. There was so much blood. *He* was there..." she slowly answered. "He said to follow his path. He said he wouldn't hurt us."

"Then let's do the opposite." Isaac flashed a reassuring smile. "We need to find a way out of this room. While I was looking for you, I couldn't find any doors or anything."

Lexie held up her arm to cast the light out further.

"We need a map." She said offhandedly.

The Anauz's light began to grow brighter and brighter until the kids could see almost every inch of the space they were in. They were standing toward the center of a huge cavern, rounded like a dome. The walls appeared to be stone, dark and smooth.

The light on Lexie's wrist began to pulse, slow at first, then faster and faster, until finally, the light retracted back in the bracelet leaving only a small radiant glow. Lexie and Isaac looked at each other.

"What was that?" Lexie asked.

"I don't kn—" was all Isaac could get out before the Anauz sent out another strong burst of light. This time it, was a solid beam pointing directly in front of them.

"Oh," Isaac said matter-of-factly, "it's a map."

"Look," Lexie said staring at the beam. "If you look straight down the light, there's something glowing. It's small."

Isaac stepped behind his sister and looked where she directed. "It's red. What do you think that means?"

"I don't know," she responded. Fixated on the object, she started moving forward. As they drew near, she could feel her heart pounding in her throat. "Cain," she whispered as she bent down and picked up the item.

"What is that?" Isaac asked.

"A diamond." Lexie held her hand out to her brother; a small white stone sat in her palm. "These are Cain's gifts to the fairies. No matter how many times I told him they were just rocks, he always said they were diamonds."

A sudden flash of clarity swept across Lexie's face. "He had a whole pocket full of these stones when he was taken! Cain was here! He's showing us the way! We'll find him!"

"Let's keep going. The way out must be close." Isaac slid the stone in his pocket.

"HEY!" The children both jumped at the word. "Give that back!"

"Who said that?" Lexie asked, searching the darkness.

"I did." The shrill little voice responded.

Lexie and Isaac looked at each other and then back to the dark. "Where are you?" they said in unison.

"Where am I? Same place I've been since you walked in. Right beside you."

With those words, there was a quiet popping sound and then the tiniest flash of white light. A small creature appeared before them, flying at eye level.

Lexie jumped back. She had never seen anything like it. The creature looked like a cross between a boy and a hummingbird. He was tiny, only six inches tall, and had wings that flapped so fast you could hardly see them. He had short blond hair and bright blue eyes that seemed to glow in the light of her bracelet.

"Are you a Fairy?" Lexie asked, a smile spreading across her face.

"Of course, child. What else would I be? You're in Fairyland," the creature responded with a hint of irritation in his voice. "Now that we all know what I am. I'm going to have to ask that you give me that stone you put in your pocket. It belongs to me."

"It's my brother's stone!" Lexie said defensively.

"You don't need to take that tone with me, child. I know who you are, I know why you're here, I know who brought the stone, and I know it was intended for me," the fairy responded. "My name is Sweyn, and I have been the happy recipient of Cain's diamonds since the very first day he started leaving them. I have found two since you got here, and that in your pocket is my third."

"Where did you find the other two?" Isaac asked.

"The first was on the fairy side of the river. The second was right by the gate. That's why I followed you in. I knew Cain was leaving them for me. I never would've come in here otherwise," Sweyn answered.

"Do you know where Elymas took him? Do you know where Cain is?" Lexie all but screamed the words.

"Elymas? Now how do you know that name?" Sweyn asked with a hint of worry in his voice.

"He told me," Lexie slowly answered.

"It makes sense," Sweyn said. "He never did like your mother. If Elymas is the one that took him, then you can trust that your brother is now with the Queen. Elymas never ventures too far from her side.

He's her most trusted council. Never understood it myself. He's not even a fairy."

"You know my mother?" Lexie asked. "And what is he, if he isn't a fairy?"

"Of course, child. I know her. Your mom is a dear friend. She used to come to Fairyland a lot when she was little. I remember playing with her on both sides of the river. I never really understood why it was so easy for her to get here, but you won't get any complaints from me. She was fun. A real breath of fresh air." Sweyn smiled.

"Those were good days. That's around the time Elymas showed up. I don't know where he came from, never much cared. I stayed out of his way, and he never was in mine. He was some old sorcerer. Had enough magic in him to pique the Queen's interest, and she must have liked what he said, because after they met, she kept him around.

"I remember your mom didn't like the look of him. She didn't like how he never stepped in the light, always sulking in shadow. She tried to talk to the Queen about it, but once Elymas had her ear, the Queen never listened to much else. Dawn never even made it to the Queen's chamber. She stopped coming around after that."

"We have to find Cain. Do you know how to get to the Queen's chamber?" Isaac asked.

"Oh, child, it's farther than you would like, I'm sure," he responded. "I haven't been there in a very long time. There are many levels. Each one has its own way of trying to deter trespassers, which is what we'll be. It's all to protect the Queen. Not sure from what. Never asked.

"I remember back when there was no gate. No castle. No levels. No need for defense. The Queen was with us. Then one day, she wasn't. It's never felt right, that gate, but then again, what do I know? I'm just a fairy. These things are much bigger than me. I'll go with you though. Help you find the boy. He's good. Plus, I need those stones."

"Why do you need them?" Lexie asked.

"Don't know, but he leaves them for me, so they must be important," Sweyn answered.

Lexie smiled. "We would be happy to have you come with us. I have a feeling we're going to need your help."

"I'll do all I can. Cain may not know me, but I know him. He's my friend," Sweyn responded. "Your fancy bangle seems to be telling you something new."

"Look at that!" Isaac exclaimed. "The light. It's changing color."

"It's not changing. It's fading. What do you think that means?" Lexie asked.

"I'm not sure, but I think we need to get out of here. This doesn't feel right," Isaac answered. "We know Cain went this way. There has to be a door or a passage somewhere."

The trio started forward, following the light as it grew dimmer. They reached the rock wall of the cavern and came to a halt.

"It's solid," Lexie said. "Why would the bracelet bring us to a solid wall?"

"Oh, child." Sweyn chuckled to himself. "I'm surprised you made it this far with that kind of mindset. On a normal day, I would laugh and say 'This is Fairyland, a place of magic,' and be done with you. But this isn't a normal day, and this isn't my Fairyland. You can't believe your eyes. You will have to use all of your senses. The magic here is strong, but you are even stronger. That's a secret we don't often share with your kind. Look past what your eyes would tell you and see things with your heart. You'll see the truth."

Lexie stepped up to the wall and placed her hand against the rock. It was cool and smooth to the touch.

"So you're saying I can see the stone, and I can feel the stone, but it's not really there?"

"Oh no, child," he responded with a smile. "It's there. What I'm saying is, it's not stone."

Sweyn flew up to the wall beside Lexie's hand. "You'll get it soon enough." With that, he flew straight through the rock face.

"Sweyn!" Lexie shouted. She turned to her brother. "I don't understand. The wall is solid." She turned back to the stone and pounded a fist against it.

Isaac stepped up beside her and placed a hand against the wall.

"I think I get it. The wall is there, but it isn't stone. It's something we can move past. The only thing holding us back is us." Isaac smiled at his sister. "Like most magic, it's an illusion. As long as we think we are trapped, we are. But as soon as we accept that, we can be free."

Isaac's hand passed into the wall, and he let out a laugh as he walked straight through.

Lexie stepped back. It didn't make any sense. How could something be there and not there at the same time? She shook her head and walked back up to the wall.

"It isn't stone. It isn't there. The only thing keeping me here is me."

With a sigh, Lexie straightened her shoulders and took a step straight into the wall and out on the other side.

# CHAPTER 5

# The Queen's Castle: Level 2

*The dragon from the ground it came*
*Seven horns each with a name*
*These things together have revealed to me*
*a future that I did not see*

Lexie gasped as she came through the wall.

"Where are we now?" she asked as she looked at her new surroundings, but no one was there to answer her.

She was standing alone on the edge of a beach. Turning, there was no sign of the wall she had just passed through. Instead, behind her, stood a deep dark wood that was so dense she didn't think she could possibly walk through without a machete. She turned back to the beach.

The sun shined so bright it was hard to believe the darkness behind her could exist. She took a step forward and realized what was happening. It took all of her strength to lift her leg. This was another dream; she was sure of it. The white sand beneath her was hot on her feet, and there was a sweet scent on the warm breeze that wrapped itself around her, like lavender and coconuts.

Lexie found herself smiling. This seemed like a very good place. The sound of waves made her laugh out loud. Just past the beach was the bluest brightest water she had ever seen. Calm waves were lapping at the sand. All of Lexie's stresses were melting away. She closed her eyes and lifted her face toward the warm sun. This is a place she could stay.

*It's beautiful, isn't it?* The voice pierced her mind.

Lexie's eyes shot open, and all the joy and peace she felt disappeared as quickly as it came. She turned to the trees behind her. Elymas stood just inside the tree line, smiling.

*This is a safe place. Just lay down in the sand. You can rest.* Elymas reassured. Slowly, he took a step out of the trees, turning her beautiful dream into a nightmare.

Storm clouds filled the sky, blocking the light and the safety it provided. The once warm breeze turned into an icy cold wind which pierced Lexie to her core. The smell of lavender disappeared and was replaced with a metallic odor.

*So beautiful.* He laughed as he took another step toward her.

Lexie turned back to the water. The tempest created giant waves that were slamming against the sand, and the once blue water now ran red. In the middle of the beach, where there was once nothing, a giant stone pillar now stood. She looked back to Elymas.

"Where is Cain?" she screamed.

Elymas stumbled backward.

"LEXIE!" She turned to the sound of Isaac shouting her name, but he wasn't there.

The wind picked up even more, howling in her ears and making it hard to see anything through the sand. She looked back at Elymas.

*Just lay down. The storm will pass. Stay here with me.* His voice echoed in her head as he reached out his hand.

"Lexie! Run!" Isaac's voice cut through the wind and hit Lexie like a jolt of electricity.

She spun around. The pillar; she had to get to the pillar. Without a second thought, she took off running. Every step more difficult than the last. The sand was pulling her down. Each step felt like hands grabbing her feet trying to hold her in place.

The wind whipped the sand into her skin, like tiny shards of glass. The pain was almost too much. She stumbled and fell to her hands and knees. She felt herself sinking into the sand. Its gritty grasp was around her legs and wrists. For the briefest moment, she thought about letting it take her.

"Lexie! Come back!"

Again, Isaac's voice brought Lexie back to the moment, and she looked up. She had fallen at the base of the pillar. With all her strength, she broke her arms free of the sand and grabbed ahold of the jagged stone. The storm continued to rage as she pulled herself up with her fingertips. She could feel the stone and sand tearing into her flesh. Her hands started to slip, and she knew the wet she felt was her own blood. With one final lunge, she pulled her feet free of the trap she was falling into and turned again to see her tormentor.

Elymas had never moved. Through the sand and the storm, Lexie could see him still standing on the edge of the beach; his earlier smile had faded to a more menacing smirk.

Despite the distance, his voice echoed in her head. *You're strong, like your mother, but I've prepared for that. We're just getting started.*

Through the sound of the storm, a deep menacing rumble, like a growl, began to grow. The ground beneath her shook, and she struggled to stay upright. Clinging to the pillar, she looked out to the raging sea. Waves of red crashed into each other, creating their own thunderous crack. As Lexie watched, a giant creature shot out of the water toward the sky like a missile. Covered in dark black scales, it spread its wings and started a downward dive toward the beach.

She was frozen. It was a dragon. An actual dragon was headed straight for her. She could see its eyes; they looked like hers—big and brown but full of hate. Four huge horns curved backward at the top of its head, and three smaller horns filled the space between. Using its tail like a rudder, the creature locked in on Lexie.

With a strength she didn't know she had, Lexie stepped forward. The chaos in her mind went suddenly silent. She could feel the Anauz pulsing against her skin, begging to be freed. Lexie shot her arm straight into the air, and a beam of radiant blue poured from her bracelet like a laser, piercing the storm clouds above and immediately dispersing them. The wind stopped, and the sun was once again revealed in its full majesty.

The light hit Elymas like a sonic wave, knocking him back into the darkness of the trees. The dragon let out a piercing howl as it veered away and disappeared, diving deep into the sea. Lexie stood triumphantly, watching as the Blanket Man scrambled to his feet.

*How did you do that?* He sneered.

With a smirk of her own, Lexie responded, "I am strong, like my mother."

Everything around her melted to black. Lexie reached out, grasping for anything in the void.

"I'm right here." She heard Isaac's voice and felt a wave of relief as his hand grabbed hers. With a yank, he pulled his sister out of the darkness of the wall.

"Are you all right?" Isaac asked, his concern obvious. "What happened? Where were you?"

"I was on a beach," she answered. "It was the most beautiful place I had ever seen. There was a storm and a dragon, and Elymas was there. I think it was just a dream."

"I wouldn't be so sure, child." Sweyn said. "You were only in the wall for a moment. As soon as Isaac came through, we heard you cry out, and he reached in for you. But look at your hands. This is dark magic."

Lexie lifted her hands. They were covered in scratches, and the blood was still dripping. There were scrapes on her arms, and she could suddenly feel the pain of everything she had just been through. To her own surprise, she didn't cry. She looked at her brother. He was staring at her wounds, and for the first time, she saw rage in his eyes.

"I'm here to protect you." Isaac shook his head in frustration. "How can I do that when this creature keeps pulling you away?"

Lexie smiled and put her hand on her brother's shoulder. "You're the only thing that has managed to pull me back. Every time I start to lose hope, I hear you. You are always with me, even when I feel alone."

A gust of wind whipped around the trio, and in the distance, a sharp howl rang out. For the first time, they looked at their new surroundings, and both children stepped back at the sight.

"What is this?" Lexie asked, looking to Sweyn who was hovering a few feet away.

"One of the original levels, child." he replied. "I've been through this before. This is the Queen's Desert. It always had a beauty to it, I thought. Though you won't feel that way in a bit."

Behind them was the wall they had just passed through. In front of them, in every other direction, there appeared to be endless dunes of sparkling sand. The light above them was a muted blue, like moonlight but with no apparent source. Isaac knelt down and scooped up a handful of sand.

"They're gemstones," he whispered as he let the colorful sand pour through his fingers.

"Oh, yes, child. Nothing but the best for our Queen. People and fairies alike could get lost in this place forever, seeking their fortune. Many have," Sweyn stated.

Another howl; this one closer.

"What is that?" Lexie asked with a twinge of fear in her voice.

"Eh, those are just wolves," Sweyn said dismissively.

"Just wolves?" Lexie gasped.

"They guard every level of the Queen's castle. You'll find them all over. They're big and scary looking, but they don't have any magic. They can't even fly." Sweyn's voice changed as the realization came to him. "But then again, neither can you. I can see why you would be scared. Now that I think of it, you should be scared. If they catch you, they'll eat you right up."

"That's very reassuring, Sweyn. Thank you," Isaac said sarcastically.

"No need for snark from you, boy. I'm just being honest," Sweyn responded. He flew a few feet out from the children and stared intently into the vast sandy abyss. "Do you see that?'

"See what?" Lexie asked, walking forward.

"A gem that sparkles brighter than the rest. There, in the distance," he responded.

"They're all sparkly," Isaac said, stepping beside his sister.

"Turn your map on, child. I would say there's a diamond ahead, and that would mark the way through."

Sweyn flew ahead, not waiting for the children.

"Hold on!" Lexie yelled as he zipped away, but he didn't listen.

She lifted her arm up, and the Anauz began to glow. A beam of light shot out showing a path that lead straight through the heart of the desert; in it, a small red beacon. Sweyn was right, Cain had been here. The children took off running the best they could, trying to catch their fairy guide.

"Sweyn wait!" they both yelled.

"Try to keep up!" Sweyn yelled over his shoulder.

He could see Cain's diamond shining bright in the distance. Suddenly, he came to a halt. The stones' light disappeared into a haze. Fear swept over him as the wind began to swirl around him. His wings beat harder and harder to try to keep him in place. He had been through this before.

Sweyn turned to the children who were trying so desperately to catch up and bellowed, "SANDSTORM!"

Both children stopped in their tracks. The wind whipped Lexie's hair into her face. She turned, thinking they could make it back to the wall and find some sort of protection, but the wall was gone. There was no sign it had ever been there; just a vast desert all around them.

The fairy peered through the sand. The storm wasn't that bad yet; every few seconds he could see a glimpse of the stone. Slowly, he started moving forward.

"Sweyn, wait, please. What do we do?" Lexie yelled out.

"I can see the diamond," he called back. "I can make it."

"Fairy!" Isaac called out.

Sweyn turned and looked at the children. Lexie was down on her knees, trying to block the sand from her eyes. Isaac was standing beside her, solid as a rock and staring directly at him.

"It's not worth your life, fairy. Come back," he said with an eerie calm that carried over the wind.

Sweyn knew he was right and started making his way back to the children. Isaac knelt down beside his sister as the fairy dropped down in front of them.

"Now what, child?" he asked. "We die together? That doesn't sound like a great plan."

"You said you had been here before," Lexie said. "What did you do then?"

"That was a very long time ago, child. I crossed the desert as fast as I could. I outflew the storm," he replied.

A wave of sand slammed into the group and whipped Sweyn into the air. Lexie reached up and caught him as Isaac stumbled backward and fell, disappearing behind the dune.

"Isaac!" Lexie screamed.

She jumped up and ran after him. Another wave of sand knocked her off balance, and she tumbled down, landing beside her brother. The sand waves were coming faster and closer together.

"Sweyn!" Lexie called out.

"I'm right here, child," his voice called back. She looked down and saw he was clinging to her shirt.

"Lexie!" Isaac yelled over top the storm. "Use the bracelet!"

Lexie looked down at the Anauz. It was glowing its brilliant blue in the darkness of the storm.

"It will be what I need," she whispered to herself. "I don't know what I need."

As suddenly as the storm started, it seemed to stop. Everything went eerily silent.

"Is it over?" Lexie asked.

"I hope so," Isaac responded.

In the distance, a wolf let out a trumpeting howl, and the entire sky came to life. The trio huddled together as lightning and thunder crashed in every direction. The wind sweeping across the desert began to swirl and pick up the tiny gemstones. Another howl, and tornados touched down all around them; seven that Lexie could make out.

She looked at her brother, he was screaming something, but she couldn't hear him over the roar of the wind and raging storm. Frustrated, Isaac pointed behind her. She turned and let out a silent scream at the sight. A wall of sand, brilliantly beautiful and deadly, was headed straight for them.

Lexie looked at her companions. A resolve overwhelmed her, drowning out all fear. She had to save them. Despite the pain of the sand against her flesh, she rose up and stood in front of Isaac and Sweyn. Positioning herself as a human shield between them and the wall of sand, a fire lit in her eyes as she lifted her arm to the storm.

"Protect us," she whispered.

The Anauz let out a deafening hum that counteracted the ringing the wind had created and then formed a shield of light in front of Lexie. The shield was the same bright blue the bracelet radiated. It was heptagon—flat on top with sharp angles leading to a pointed bottom and tall enough to cover a grown man.

"Us!" Lexie screamed, and the shield immediately expanded, encompassing all three travelers in a glowing orb.

From the safety of their new force field, they could see the storm outside as it carried on, but inside, it was silent and calm. Lexie sat down beside her brother and Sweyn.

"So I guess we just wait it out," she said to break the silence.

"That would be wise, child. Your magic seems to have sparked an interest," Sweyn stated as he nodded past Lexie.

Both children turned and peered into the storm; looking back were three sets of very large eyes, glowing a muted purple. Unnatural and almost beautiful if it weren't for the malice they easily conveyed.

"Wolves?" Isaac quietly asked.

"That would be them, child," he said with a hint of defeat in his voice. "And now they have seen us."

Lexie continued to watch the eyes as Isaac and Sweyn carried on behind her. Slowly, she made her way to the edge of the orb as one set of eyes did the exact same. Now only inches apart, Lexie could see the beast in all its terrifying glory. It stood four feet tall at the shoulder, at least seven feet in length not counting its massive tail. Its fur was the purest black. Though she couldn't hear it through the shield, Lexie was certain the beast was growling. Its disproportionately large head was lowered ever so slightly, and she could see the fur along its back was standing straight up.

Lexie eased her way back to the others. At this point, they had stopped their back and forth and were watching the interaction.

Lexie sat down as the giant wolf lowered himself to the ground outside. It seemed a battle of wills was underway; neither the girl nor the beast willing to break eye contact, when a sound in the distance forced them both to look away.

Through the sand and wind of the storm, another wolf came into view. It was easy to spot with its bright white fur. Despite the distance, it was easy to tell this wolf was even larger than those outside the sphere. It let out a bellowing howl that echoed even inside their dome of safety. The winds began to slow, and the sand started to settle back into place. The white wolf turned and disappeared over its distant dune. Lexie looked back to the wolf that was outside the orb, but there was no trace of it or its counterparts.

After a few moments, the force field around them faded away into nothing, and they were exposed to the sands once again. Everything was calm and glittering, as if the storm had never happened.

"What just happened?" Lexie asked, looking to Sweyn.

"I have never seen that before, nor do I care to again, child," he answered. "Let's just get through this desert before any of that has a chance to repeat itself."

Lexie lifted her arm, and the beam of light that was guiding them shined out once again, pointing them over a nearby dune. As fast as they could manage, they made their way through the sand, following the light. On the other side of the dune was a large round wooden door that led into the sandy floor.

"Ah, that's a way out, if I've ever seen one," Sweyn stated as he landed on the wooden planks.

There were no windows or ornate markings; it was plain door with a large iron handle and a knotted rope attached to it. The children grabbed ahold of the rope and pulled together. It took all their strength, but slowly, the door creaked open. After they passed the halfway point, it slammed into the sand with a muted thud, sending gemstone flying in every direction.

The trio peeked over the edge. The opening seemed to lead straight down into a vast abyss. The only thing visible was a single rope that descended into the darkness. Lexie and Isaac stepped back.

"I don't like it," Isaac stated. "Maybe double check."

Lexie agreed and pulled out her bracelet.

"Which way?" she asked and then sighed at the response.

The light shined straight down into the pit before them.

With a sideways glance, Lexie looked at her brother. "Gentlemen first?"

"I'm pretty sure that's not the saying, but okay."

Isaac threw his legs over the side of the ledge and grabbed ahold of the rope. Slowly, he lowered himself down. There were knots in the rope which made everything easier.

After he was a few feet down, he yelled up to his sister. "Okay, Lexie, come on down. It isn't so bad."

Lexie looked over the edge. She could barely see her brother as he disappeared into the darkness. With a sigh, she grabbed the rope and began her descent.

"Don't worry, child. I'll stay right here beside you," Sweyn said as he fluttered a few inches away.

Lexie smiled at him as she climbed down. But her smile quickly faded as she heard a creaking sound above them and looked up just in time to see the massive door slam closed overhead.

Panic began to seep in as Lexie closed her eyes and held tightly to the rope, too terrified to move.

"Come on, Lexie, just keep moving. We can do this!" Isaac called from below her. He seemed so far away.

Hesitantly, Lexie opened her eyes and looked down, hoping for a glimpse of her brother. But in the darkness, she couldn't see anything, just the rope.

"Keep moving, child," Sweyn said as he came into view. "Don't look down. Just keep going."

Lexie nodded and started lowering herself inch by inch down the rope. The rope itself was very thick; it seemed old and strong. It was very rough, and each time she moved her hands down, it became more painful to hold on. Her earlier wounds were tearing open again; she could feel the blood running down her arms.

Without warning, Lexie's strength gave out. She clamored to grab ahold of the rope, but it was too late. She was falling. She could see Sweyn diving after her. But she was falling too fast, he couldn't catch up. She zipped past Isaac as he screamed her name.

In a flash, he was gone, Sweyn was gone. All that was left was the rope. Each time she tried to grab it, it ripped at her skin, and she couldn't hold on. This was it. She was almost at the bottom, and she could sense it. She closed her eyes and readied for the impact, but it never came.

Lexie realized she was no longer falling. She opened her eyes, and she was standing in the middle of a road. There was something about it she recognized—something from a distant memory.

*Welcome back.* The familiar voice echoed in her mind.

"Not again." Lexie sighed to herself as she turned to face her tormentor.

# CHAPTER 6

# The Queen's Castle: Level 3

*It's ten past ten, and this room is growing cold*
*The candle's burning down, and the dark is getting bold*
*I see the sudden flashes of light, hear the voices in the wall*
*They say so many things to me, but all I hear is 'Don't Fall'*

Dawn walked into her empty house. She could hear Alex outside screaming into his phone. Soon, there would be a hundred people outside—police, EMTs, search parties, everyone. How did she explain that they wouldn't find the kids? How could she tell their father where they actually were? No one would believe her. She barely believed herself, and she had spent so much time there.

Slowly, she made her way to her bedroom, locking the door behind her. She picked up a picture of Lexie and Cain and fell onto her bed. Through silent sobs, she whispered their names and laid her hand on the picture; without thought, she closed her eyes.

A warm breeze caressed her face. Dawn opened her eyes, and she was standing on the road in front of her grandparents' house. She hadn't been here in years. The sun was shining bright and warm. She smiled as the light surrounded her. Another breeze filled with the scent of roses and wildflowers pushed the hair away from her eyes.

*Welcome back.* A dark voice echoed in her mind. A voice she knew all too well. A voice she knew wasn't directed at her.

Dawn turned away from the house and started running down the road, toward the shadows, where the road turned sharply into the woods.

"And where are we now?" Dawn heard her daughter ask. Her heart skipped a beat and then dropped into the pit of her stomach as she rounded the turn and saw her baby girl standing ten feet away from pure evil.

*Nowhere special.* His voice rang inside both their minds. *Just another step in the journey. You're still so far away. Cain doesn't have much time left. If you would like, I could take you to him.*

Elymas stepped forward; his long limbs putting him nearly within reach of Lexie. He reached out his hand. Lexie looked at him for a moment. Could it be that easy?

Neither of them seemed to notice Dawn approaching.

"Get away from her, sorcerer!" She commanded.

The words hit Elymas like a train, and he stumbled backward, falling against a tree.

Lexie spun around and saw her mother standing just a few feet behind her. She couldn't control the wave of emotion that tore through her. Tears started streaming down her face as she ran into her mother's outstretched arms. All of the fear and anger and stress of what she had been through melted away; in that moment, she knew she was safe.

Dawn held her daughter tightly against her chest but never took her eyes off Elymas. Walking backward, he slowly disappeared into the trees.

Lexie pulled back from her mother and looked up into her eyes.

"How are you here?" she asked as the tears continued to pour.

"Aww, baby, you are part of me," Dawn responded. "I am part of you. I'm always with you, and this is a place of the most beautiful kind of magic."

Lexie looked around. "Where did he go?"

"Away, for now, but until your task is complete, he'll keep showing up, trying to lead you off the right path," Dawn answered as she started walking down the road, back from where she had come.

Lexie scrambled to catch up. "Where are we going?" she asked.

"This is a very special place to me. I want you to see it before we run out of time." Dawn smiled at the thought of what was ahead.

As they rounded the sharp turn in the road, Lexie let out a gasp and stopped in her tracks.

"I know this place!" she said excitedly. "I've been here, but... something's different."

Lexie let the moment overtake her. The sun was shining so bright as far as she could see, and the warmth of it felt so comforting. Along the road were the most vibrantly colored wildflowers, and the scent they let out was the most wonderful thing she had ever smelled—like lavender and cinnamon rolls and pumpkin pie all mixed together. In the distance, she could hear some music; it was faint, but happy. She could also hear a light rapping, like metal against metal.

Dawns' smile turned into an audible laugh. "Yes, my love. You have been to a version of this place. You see that little house up ahead? That is the home of your great-grandparents."

The reunited duo continued down the road, headed straight for the house. Dawn stopped at a grouping of hanging baskets over-flowing with beautiful flowers, the most vibrant pinks and red Lexie had ever seen. As Dawn leaned in and smelled the blooms, the joy of it almost overwhelmed her. Tears filled her eyes as she turned to her daughter.

"My grandmother always loved flowers," she said.

"Where, exactly, are we?" Lexie asked as she looked around. "You said I've been to a version of this place. What does that mean?"

A loud metal clang rang out from the other side of the house, and Lexie could hear someone muttering under their breath.

"I'll show you," Dawn said.

Smiling, she took her daughter's hand and led her around house. There was a long smooth driveway that led past the large back porch to a garage. The garage door was open, and there was an old truck sticking halfway out with the hood propped up. Inside, they could hear tools rattling around and someone grumbling. As they made their way down the driveway, the scent of freshly baked bread drifted out to meet them.

"Hope you're hungry, girls!" a sweet voice called out. "I've been baking all day."

Dawn's joy couldn't be held back any longer, "Nanny!" she called out as she took off running to the porch.

A young woman was standing there to greet her. Dawn threw her arms around the woman's neck as she let out the sweetest laugh.

"You always make such a fuss when you come to visit," the young woman proclaimed.

Lexie watched the interaction, completely baffled. The two women were talking and laughing like old friends. She had heard her mom tell stories about her grandparents, but this couldn't be the woman Dawn fondly referred to as Nanny; she looked even younger than her mom. Standing side by side, the young woman was at least six inches shorter than her mom, with long curly black hair and a small frame. It didn't make any sense.

"Lexie," Dawn called out, "come meet your great-grandmother."

The woman turned her attention to Lexie as she started up the steps to the porch. For the first time, Lexie could see her eyes. Though age didn't reach her face, her bright grey eyes seemed nearly ancient in the wisdom they carried. Although she knew the woman was looking at her, it felt more like she could see through her. In that moment, Lexie felt very small.

"I have always known you," the woman said, smiling at Lexie. "My beautiful Alexandria. Welcome to our home. My name is Isola."

Out of the garage, another loud bang rang out followed by the increasingly familiar grumbling.

Lexie laughed out loud and turned to her mother. "He sounds like Papaw."

Dawn let out a laugh of her own. "You have no idea," she said.

"Elms!" their hostess cried out. "Stop muttering to yourself and come out here. We have company!"

Lexie stared at the garage door as a giant of a man emerged. He was at least six foot four inches and very strong. His dark brown hair was just long enough to fall into his eyes, which were the same bright grey as the woman's. He smiled a big broad smile as he approached the porch and held out his hand to Lexie.

"Name's Elmis," he said, still smiling, "but you can call me Pap."

Lexie took his hand, and he gave her a hearty shake that made her laugh as she looked back to her mother. "And this is your great-grandfather."

Dawn laughed.

"How is this possible?" Lexie asked, turning to her mother. "Where are we?"

"This is a very special part of Fairyland," Dawn answered. "This is a place of peace. Only good magic is here. A place of pure light."

"Are you fairies?" Lexie asked her great-grandparents who were now standing side by side holding hands.

"Oh no," Elmis responded as they both laughed. "We're just servants of the light. This is our paradise."

"Everyone, have a seat," Isola said, motioning to the table and chairs behind them, "I'll get us all some cake."

"I'm sorry, Nanny, but we can't stay," Dawn said with a deep regret in her voice. "The sorcerer has taken Cain to the Queen."

All the joy melted from their faces as Isola took both of Lexie's hands into hers. Looking down at them, she could see the evidence of the pain the girl had already endured.

"The light that created this place is inside you. You have more strength and power than you can possibly imagine. Even in the darkest parts of the Queen's Castle, your light will remain. Do not fear. Do not question your heart. Use the power you have been given. Have faith, and you will save your brother."

Isola released Lexie's hands, and Dawn wrapped her arms around her daughter, pulling her in so tight she could barely breathe.

"I love you so much," she said as she eased her hold on Lexie and pulled back so she could see in her eyes. A tear ran down Dawn's cheek. "I am always with you."

The beautiful world around them quickly faded to black.

"Mom!" Lexie cried out, but it was too late. She was standing on a stone boulder. All she could see in the dim light was the bottom of a rope dangling in front of her.

"Lexie!" She heard Isaac yell from above. Looking up, she could barely make out his silhouette descending the rope.

Sweyn zipped down and lifted a flower petal off Lexie's shoulder. "And now, where might you have been, child?" he asked with a knowing twinkle in his eye.

Isaac hopped off the rope and landed right in front of her. The expression on his face shifting from worry to joy.

"I was with Mom," she said with a smile as the memory of what she had just experienced washed over her.

Before she could say anything else, the ground beneath their feet began to shake. Isaac grabbed ahold of Lexie's arm as the boulder they were standing on split in two. A thunderous roar echoed in the distance, and the tremors increased tenfold.

"We have to get out of here!" Isaac screamed over the growing chaos. "Which way?"

Lexie was clinging onto Isaac as she lifted her arm. The Anauz sprang to life, and a path was highlighted to their right.

"There," she yelled back to her brother. "It must be the way out."

As quickly as they could, the children scrambled down off the boulder and landed on a stone floor. The only light was what came from the bracelet. The ground beneath them was shaking violently. Lexie and Isaac clung to each other as they slowly made their way forward.

Sweyn landed on Lexie's shoulder and held tightly on to her shirt.

"We have to move faster, child," he yelled into her ear. "Things are about to get really bad!"

At that moment, the floor all around them began to splinter and crack like glass under too much pressure.

"Run!" he screamed.

The children didn't need any more encouragement; both were in a full sprint following the path the bracelet laid out.

"There it is!" Isaac yelled, pointing in front of them.

Lexie could see it. It looked like a hallway cut into solid stone. Inside, a small light was flickering. With the ground crumbling behind them, the trio passed over the threshold of the hallway and stumbled to the ground. A metal door came crashing down behind them and, with its seal, came a deafening silence.

Both children laid on the ground where they had fallen, gasping for air. Sweyn flew up into the air.

"This is new," he said. "I've never been here." There was a noticeable hesitation in his voice.

Lexie and Isaac slowly clamored to their feet. They were in a very long dark hallway, lit by a single fiery lantern dangling a few feet in front of them. The ceiling was only a foot above their heads, and they could barely stand side by side. Isaac laid his hand on the stone wall.

"It's warm," he said.

Sweyn repeated his action. "I don't like it, child," he nearly whispered.

Lexie walked forward until she was under the lantern and leaned into the unknown, peering into the seemingly endless darkness in front of them. As she waited for her eyes to adjust, she could hear something moving ahead of them.

"Something is in here," she said.

As soon as the words left her mouth, there was a huff of noise that made them all step backward and then the terrifying sound of something running toward them. The footfalls grew louder as the creature approached and then, suddenly, fell silent. The children desperately searched the darkness. At the very edge of the light, they could just make out the creatures' eyes. Eyes they had seen before. It was one of the wolves that had hunted them in the sandstorm.

The beast lowered its head, and with a deep menacing growl, it stepped slowly into the light. Lexie turned to run, but Isaac was standing in her path, a very clear anger on his face. He stepped around his sister and placed himself between her and the wolf. Lexie watched in horror as the two moved within a few feet of each other.

"Leave." Isaac commanded.

The wolf flashed its teeth as it snarled and took a step closer.

Isaac matched its move.

"You have no place in the light," he whispered as a knowing smile crossed his lips.

The wolf hesitantly took another step forward. His demeanor more anxious now than menacing. Isaac reached up and plucked the lantern from the ceiling, shifting the light in the passageway. The wolf froze in place as Isaac reached into the lantern and pulled the flame out with his bare hands. The light swept around his fingers like water and began to grow bigger and brighter as Isaac stepped forward.

"Tell your master, the light is here," he said in proclamation. "Now!"

The wolf yelped and, in a flash, disappeared into the wall of the passage. The flame in Isaac's hand lowered down to its original brightness as he placed it back inside the glass of the lantern. Slowly, he turned to face his counterparts.

Lexie and Sweyn were both staring at him in disbelief.

"What was that?" Lexie nearly shouted.

"That was magic," Sweyn said with a smile on his face, "the purest magic. You have the power of light. You're a fairy?"

"Not a fairy." Isaac laughed as he shook his head. "Just a servant of the light."

Before they could ask any more questions, the environment of the passageway began to shift. The stone surrounding them creaked and moaned as the air became frigid.

"What's happening?" Lexie asked, her breath freezing in the air as it left her mouth.

"Come, children." Sweyn urged. "We must move quickly. Only the presence of an Elemental could effect this drastic a change."

"What's an Elemental?" Lexie whispered through her shivers.

"Another of the Queen's guard, child. One we're not prepared to meet." He hurriedly responded, "Now, you really must run."

The children took off down the passage, straight into the unknown darkness.

"Just stick together!" Sweyn called back over his shoulder. He couldn't be more than a few feet in front of them, but to Lexie he sounded a mile away.

She kept running, occasionally bumping the side of the stone wall. She could hear Isaac right in front of her, but the light of the lantern was far behind them. The tunnel seemed never ending. Her terror began to grow as she ran deeper and deeper into the darkness.

"Isaac!" she called out when she realized she couldn't hear him anymore.

Silence.

"Isaac!" she screamed as she slowed to a stop. "Sweyn!"

No response.

She threw her arms out in front of her and grasped for the wall she knew was so close, but nothing was there. In total darkness, she began to frantically spin, throwing herself in every direction, but there was nothing to stop her. Slowly, she lowered herself down to the ground and began to crawl. At least, the ground offered her some comfort.

Tears streamed down her face as she made her way forward, inch by inch. After a few moments, the stone beneath her fingers began to transform, Lexie realized she was no longer on rock but something that felt more like grass. Soft and warm. She leaned her face down closer to the ground and took in a deep breath. It was grass and dirt. She wasn't in the tunnel any longer.

With a blinding flash of light, the world around her came to life. She definitely wasn't in the stone passageway any more. She wasn't even sure she was in Fairyland anymore. She stood up and looked around; she was standing in a clearing in the middle of the woods. The trees were big and old. The warm sun was a welcome change from the cold of the passage, but the colors here seemed muted—like she was looking at the world through a fog. She could hear birds singing and bees buzzing, but she knew that something was wrong. She wasn't supposed to be here.

"Hello." A small voice echoed behind her.

Lexie turned to see a small girl standing in front of her, and a cold chill ran down her spine.

"Are you lost?" the girl asked. "Do you need help?"

"Mom?" Lexie whispered.

# CHAPTER 7

# The Woods: Part 2

*I dream the dreams both day and night*
*of wolves who dawn both black and white*
*In groups of three they come to me*
*the meaning of which only now I see*

"Mom?" The girl let out a light-hearted laugh. "Did you hit your head? I'm not your mom. I'm Dawn. I live just down the hill. Are you all right? Do you need me to call someone for you?"

Lexie just stared at the girl in disbelief. It was her mom, but she couldn't have been more than ten or eleven. Her long hair was tied up on top of her head in a messy bun, and she had on an old sweatshirt and jeans that fit her thin frame very awkwardly.

"I'm okay," she finally responded. "I'm sorry, I think I'm just lost. I'm Lexie."

"It's easy to get lost out here," Dawn said as she started to walk toward the trees. "Come with me, I'll help you get back home."

"Thank you," Lexie hesitantly responded as she followed the girl toward the tree line.

"Wait!" Dawn said stopping in her tracks and spinning around to face Lexie. "I know you! You're the girl I saw! My mom and I were talking to a woman in the woods, and you were there!"

"No!" Lexie quickly quipped. "Well, yes, but no."

Dawn stared at Lexie in confusion.

"Yes, I was there," Lexie continued, "but I wasn't supposed to be."

"And you could see the woman!?" Dawn excitedly asked.

"Yes," Lexie answered, "I could see all three of you."

Dawn did an excited little dance, and Lexie couldn't help but laugh out loud; her mom still did that dance whenever she got happy. It was so bizarre to see her this way—to see the child her mother used to be.

"You have to meet my mom!" Dawn said with a huge smile on her face.

She reached out and grabbed Lexie's hand and took off toward the trees at a half run. Lexie struggled to keep up without falling. Dawn obviously knew the ground really well, but Lexie seemed to trip over every root and dip. As they crossed into the trees, Lexie could see a well-worn path that snaked its way down the hill. Suddenly, Lexie stopped in her tracks, halting Dawn.

"I know this story," Lexie said as she looked around the woods. "You've told me this story. I thought you made it up."

"What are you talking about?" Dawn asked, letting go of Lexie's hand and taking a step back.

"When I was little, you told me this story. You told me about the girl you met in the woods, the one who saved you from the monsters then disappeared."

Lexie took in a deep breath and tried to calm herself down.

"I've never told you any stories," Dawn replied as a wave of worry washed over her face. "I don't know you."

"You don't know me now, but one day, you will." Lexie looked up to the treetops and began to sweep the skyline. "I can't explain it right now, but we need to get out of here. It isn't safe!"

"What do you mean it isn't safe? I've been here all my life. There's nothing to be afraid of." Dawn took another step away from Lexie.

"You don't understand, I know how this ends. We need to go. Now!" Lexie reached out and took Dawn's hand just as a piercing howl rang out in the distance.

"What is that?" Dawn screamed.

"Wolves!" Lexie yelled back. "RUN!"

The girls took off through the woods; Lexie practically dragging Dawn down the hill.

"Wait!" Dawn yelled. "Just stop!"

Lexie came to a sudden halt, desperately trying to catch her breath as she searched the woods, looking for the source of her fears. Dawn fell down to the ground, panting.

"There are no wolves here," she said through her gasps. "What is happening?"

Lexie looked down at her young mother and saw a thick fog rising out of the ground. Dawn jumped up in a panic.

"What is this?" she whispered, looking to Lexie for guidance. "Who are you?"

A low growl let out just feet away; the fog was so thick and rising so quickly Lexie couldn't see anything below it.

"Get behind me!" She shouted to Dawn, who did so without question.

"They're here," she whispered.

The two girls stood back to back, slowly circling and scanning the ground for any sign of the wolves. Aside from the fog, which oozed and pulsed as if it were itself alive, there was no movement in the woods. The birds were no longer singing, and even the wind had stopped blowing.

Lexie quickly searched her mind for the memory of the story. Her mom had told her this story a dozen times; she gave every detail. Lexie only ever half listened because it was just one of her mom's many tales. She never thought it could be true. More than that, she never thought one day her life might depend on it.

All at once, the details came flooding through her mind. The mystery girl, the fog, the cave, the wolves, the sword. The sword. Lexie smiled as she replayed her mother's words over and over. Quickly she grabbed Dawn's hand and took off running down the hill but not on the path that was laid out. Despite the fog and foreign terrain, she quickened her pace; she knew where they were going.

"No!" Dawn yelled as she stumbled over unseen rocks and roots. "Not this way, this doesn't lead home!"

"I know," Lexie called back, "but this is where you said to go!"

"This is dangerous. There's a drop!" Dawn tried to stop Lexie, but it was too late. Without warning the two went toppling down a steep embankment, disappearing into the fog.

Lexie lost ahold of Dawn's hand as she rolled down the hill, hitting her arm against a tree and ripping her jeans. None of that shook her resolve though; she had to protect Dawn. As soon as she reached the bottom, she was back up on her feet. The fog was so thick she couldn't see more than a few feet in front of her.

"Dawn!" she called out.

"I'm over here." Her mother's small voice came back.

Slowly, Lexie made her way to where her young mother stood, back against a tree and eyes full of terror.

"Please, tell me what's happening," Dawn whispered. "Is this a nightmare? I don't know where we are."

"Not a nightmare," Lexie whispered back. "Everything will be okay, I promise."

Lexie stepped closer to Dawn, and she could hear the sound of water dripping in the distance. "This way."

Carefully, they made their way to what looked like a small cave. This was it. This is what Dawn had described to Lexie so many times before. This is where her mother and the mystery girl made their stand against the wolves. This is where they would fight. This is where they would win.

There was a rustle of noise behind them; both girls spun around to face whatever might step out of the fog. The eyes were the first thing they saw, two sets of large menacing eyes. Together, the wolves slowly stepped out of the fog, revealing their full terrifying majesty to the girls. Lexie looked closely into the eyes of the wolf in front of her. It was the same creature she saw in the sandstorm.

"I know you," she said. "I've seen you."

"They're us," Dawn said with resolution in her voice.

Lexie looked over at Dawn and saw that she was inches away from the second wolf. It stood just as tall as her, and they were staring into each other's eyes.

"What do you mean, 'they're us'?" Lexie said as she looked back to her wolf, which was now just as close as the other.

"Look into its eyes," Dawn said. "You'll see a reflection of your own anger. It's an old magic. The best defense."

Slowly, she reached her hand out and grabbed Lexie's arm, never taking her eyes off the wolf. "Get behind me."

"No," Lexie said matter-of-factly. "I know what happens next."

At that moment, a loud howl rang out in the distance. Both wolves stepped back, lowering their heads. They began to growl as they moved together to attack.

Lexie stepped in front of Dawn and lifted her arm in defense. The Anauz began to pulse and glow as the end of her arm became a sword of light.

"Stay behind me," Lexie called over her shoulder.

"Not a chance," Dawn replied.

Lexie looked back as her young mother stepped up to her side, wielding a matching sword. Simultaneously, the wolves lunged at the girls, each dodging the attack and swinging their swords without mercy.

The wolf attacking Lexie yelped in pain as she swiped its side with her blade. Another howl from the distance called the attack off. Lexie watched as her wolf disappeared into the fog. Turning, she saw Dawn kneeling over the second wolf. Tears were streaming down her face as a puddle of blood formed around the beast she had just slain.

Dawn looked up at the girl who had shown up out of nowhere, who tried to protect her, who fought beside her.

"You came here from Fairyland?" she asked.

"Yes," Lexie replied.

"You have the Anauz?" Dawn asked.

"I do," Lexie said.

Dawn rose up from the ground and looked toward the sky. Raising her arm as high as she could, she whispered something under her breath. A bright beam of light, blinding and pure, shot out from her bracelet, and the fog lifted from the ground, taking the slain wolf with it. In a moment, everything was as it once had been. The sun was shining bright, birds were happily chirping, and a warm breeze swept through the air.

Dawn turned her gaze back to Lexie. "How?"

"How what?" Lexie asked.

"How did you get here from Fairyland? How did you get to Fairyland to begin with?" Dawn asked as she started moving toward Lexie. "How do we have the same bracelet? How do you know me? How did you know where to go and what was going to happen?"

Lexie looked at Dawn. She may be younger than the mother she knew, but the eyes were the same. That all-knowing wisdom she had always found so interesting was already there. Looking at her now, Lexie knew she already had the answer.

Lexie just smiled. "Because you told me, Mom."

With that, the world around her faded to black. Lexie closed her eyes and waited for the moment to pass. Where would she be when she opened her eyes again? At this point, it could be anywhere. Cautiously, she opened her eyes. This, definitely, is not what she expected.

In front of her, sitting in what looked like a glass cube, sat Cain. Tears were streaming down his face.

Carefully, Lexie eased her way toward her little brother. The room she was in seemed very similar to the entrance to the castle. It was dark, but an ambient red glow radiated from the edges of the floor. The light seemed to move like water along the stone walls. From the center of the domed ceiling, a blinding ray of white light shot straight down and illuminated the cube.

Aside from Cain, the room seemed to be empty.

"Cain," Lexie whispered as she approached the glass enclosure.

"Lexie!" Cain shouted.

He jumped up, nearly hitting his head on the top of his cell, and started looking in every direction. He went to each side of the cube and pressed his hands to the glass over his eyes, squinting into the dark. The light surrounding him was too bright; he couldn't see anything.

"Lexie!" he cried out again.

"Shhh!" She hushed. "I'm here!"

Lexie pressed her hand to the glass right in front of Cain's. Tears filled his eyes as she came into view.

"I'm here," she said again, this time more reassuringly. "I'm going to get you out of here."

"It doesn't open, and I can't break it," Cain said as Lexie began to search the surface of the cube for any weakness. "How did you get here?"

"I don't know," she responded, running her hands around the edges of the glass. "After the rope and the boulder, I was with Isaac and Sweyn in a stone tunnel. Then I was in the past talking to Mom when she was a kid, then I was here."

For a moment, Cain simply stared at her.

Without stopping her inspection of the cube, she looked at her brother. She could see all the questions running through his mind. Cain had always been doubtful. No matter what she said, he had a dozen questions. Plus, he never got carried away in their Mom's stories the way she did. He would listen, but even with her, he would have questions regarding the validity of the stories. General questions about the physics associated with what she was saying and more specific questions which seemed designed to tear any story apart. He began to speak, and she prepared herself for the onslaught.

"You aren't actually here," he said.

Lexie let out a little laugh. "Of course, I am, and I'm going to get you out."

"No," Cain said very matter-of-factly. "If you were in the tunnel last, then you have five more levels to go before you actually get here."

"No!" Lexie said, desperation growing in her voice, "I'm here! I have to be here!"

"Listen to me," he said with urgency. "Every story mom ever told us is true. You have to go through so much more before you get here."

Cain paused and looked away for a moment. "Go back," he whispered.

Lexie stopped her desperate search of the cube and looked at her brother, tears filling her eyes.

"Go back home. I'll be okay, don't come here—"

"It's my fault you're here." Lexie said. "And I'm going to save you."

A loud clanging sound radiated through the cavernous room.

"It's coming!" Cain shouted. "Get out now! Go home!"

Lexie desperately looked around the room trying to find the source of the sound.

"What is it? What's coming!?"

"The Elemental! Run!" he screamed.

Lexie turned to run but there, behind her, rose a huge three-headed snake. Each head seemed to move independent of the others. The first head looked like a cobra. It was a dark red, like blood, and the hood that surrounded its face was as black as night; its eyes smoldered like fresh embers, and as it breathed, small sparks of fire shot out of its nostrils. The second head, which looked more like a python, was a pale jaundiced yellow. When its monstrous tongue flickered out of its mouth, it brought with it arcs of electricity. The third and final head was that of a dragon, as white as snow, with pale blue eyes. This head stayed closer to the ground, and as it moved, the ground beneath it began to freeze. All three patterns swirled together where the heads met to make one beautiful and terrifying creature.

Lexie stumbled backward and turned to see her brother—a look of terror frozen on his face.

A new wave of strength washed over her as she looked at Cain, quickly turning her fear to empowered resolve. She pressed her hand to the glass and looked deep into Cain's eyes.

As the monster advanced, she leaned in as close to the glass as she could and whispered, "I'm coming back for you."

With that, she was gone. She disappeared as though she had never been there. Cain watched as the snake searched the room for his sister. He sat down in the middle of his prison, and a smile spread across his face. She said she was coming back. He knew she would.

# CHAPTER 8

# The Queen's Castle: Level 4

*When you look into the mirror, what do you see?*
*When I look into the mirror, I see everything but me*
*I see a way I did not look; I see a path I did not take*
*I see a tear I did not shed; I see a smile I did not fake*

Lexie felt a wave of nausea as she opened her eyes. Disoriented and heartbroken, she took in her new surroundings. It was a cave that seemed to lead even deeper into the ground. Ahead, the dim light of a small fire was flickering, and she could hear hushed voices locked into a heated argument.

Pushing herself against the side of the cave, she slowly and stealthily began to make her way toward the light. Once she was close enough to make out what was being said, she let out a huge sigh of relief that culminated in an audible laugh.

The voices immediately fell silent, and Lexie watched as Isaac and Sweyn threw themselves on the ground.

"It's too late," she said with a smile as she stepped into the light. "You've been discovered."

Isaac jumped up from the ground and ran to Lexie.

"Where have you been? We've been searching for you for hours! We thought the worst had happened."

"I fought wolves with the child version of our mother then went to see Cain," Lexie said as tears filled her eyes. "He's being kept in a solid stone cavern inside an impenetrable glass cube, protected by a giant three-headed snake that breathes fire, electricity, and ice."

Isaac stepped back, and Lexie could see the concern in his eyes.

"He told me to go home," Lexie said, just above a whisper. "He said to leave him." Her tears now streamed down her face.

"I can't! I did this to him!" She cried out through her sobs. "He's innocent! He didn't do anything wrong! I didn't do anything wrong! How could Elymas do this to us!? What did we do to deserve this?"

Lexie doubled over as the sobs overwhelmed her, making it impossible to speak. Isaac and Sweyn watched silently as she fell to her knees. They both knew where her mind was headed.

As her tears slowed, so did her breathing. Carefully, she lifted herself up from the ground and looked Isaac straight in the eyes. He could see the anger. He could see the rage. The Anauz on Lexie's wrist began to glow, but she didn't seem to notice.

"I hate him." Lexie seethed.

As the words left her mouth, her bracelet shot out a blinding light that knocked Isaac and Sweyn to the ground. Lexie turned her face away and covered her eyes with her other arm. The light pulled back in on itself, and the three travelers watched in awe as the light moved up Lexie's arm and over her chest. The light enveloped her, and she could feel its warmth pulsing through her body.

Isaac scrambled to his feet and watched as the light lifted Lexie off the ground. His sister threw her head back and couldn't hold in the joyous laughter that poured out. A small smile crossed his lips as she slowly lowered back to the ground. The light began to fade, lingering for a moment right over her heart, then disappeared completely.

Lexie turned to Isaac.

"What was that?" she asked with a huge smile still painted on her face.

"I told you before," he replied, "the Anauz will be anything you need it to be. Your heart was headed down a dark and poisonous road. The Anauz simply reminded it of the light. It will shield your heart as long as you allow it. It will protect you, even from yourself."

Lexie let out a long sigh of relief and let the tension in her neck and shoulders melt away.

"Okay then. Now that that's over, where are we?"

Isaac's smile grew wider, and the light in his eyes seemed to sparkle a little as he responded, "We are definitely in a cave!"

Lexie let out a small laugh as she lowered herself down beside the fire. She hadn't realized she was cold until now.

"Funny," she said sarcastically. "What I meant to ask is, Sweyn, have you been here before, and do you know the way out?"

Sweyn flew over to Lexie and landed at her side.

"I'm sorry, child, I've never seen this. Under any other circumstances I wouldn't care to. I knew things had changed down here over the years. I didn't realize just how much. I couldn't begin to guess how much further we have to go."

"Five levels," Lexie said solemnly. "Cain said if we were in the tunnels, then we had five more levels until we got to him."

Isaac sat down across the fire from Lexie and Sweyn. "We should rest here for a while. Try to get some sleep."

"I can't sleep." Lexie began to argue. "I promised Cain I would be back for him. He's alone, surrounded by monsters, and he's so afraid. We have to get to him as fast as we can—"

"The boy is right." Sweyn cut in. "You're exhausted. You'll be no good to us or Cain if you don't rest. Don't worry, child. I'll watch over you."

Lexie gave in. She understood their argument. Reluctantly, she curled up beside the fire.

"Only for a little bit, okay?"

"You have my word, child. Now sleep."

As the words left his mouth, Lexie closed her eyes, and in a moment, she was sound asleep.

"You didn't have to use magic on her," Isaac said with a smile.

"We both know I did," he responded with a laugh.

Isaac stared at his sister as she slept.

"The deeper we go, the more difficult everything will get. I'm worried about her."

Sweyn nodded his head in agreement. "This isn't a task for the weak, but in case you haven't noticed, she's anything but weak. It's natural to worry about the ones we love, child, and I know this is your first time in the dark, but she's been staring it down since birth. She is so much stronger than any of us realize. Good and bad alike."

Isaac settled his back against a rock. "I've never slept before," he said as he leaned his head back and closed his eyes.

"Well then, child, you are in for a treat. For many people, it's their very favorite pastime." With a wave of his hand, Isaac was asleep.

Sweyn looked around the tunnel, then back to his travelling companions. He could see the weariness and worry lifting from them as they slept. He could hear the resolve of their mother beating in their chests. He knew part of her was here, watching over them as well. Satisfied, he took up a sentry post on the highest rock above the children.

Isaac opened his eyes. He wasn't in the tunnel. Panic began to set in as he tried to get his bearings. Where was Lexie? Where was Sweyn? Isaac took a step forward, and the world around him came into focus. He was in a dark room; there was moonlight pouring in through the window. Slowly, he pulled the curtains back and looked out. This was Lexie's house. This must be her room. How did he get here?

"When you look into the mirror, what do you see?"

Isaac spun around to see his mother standing in the doorway.

"What?" he asked as he started toward her.

"When you look into the mirror, what do you see?" Dawn repeated.

"I don't understand. Where am I?" Isaac asked, stopping right in front of his mother.

"This is just a dream, my love. You're still in the tunnel with your sister, but I am here to warn you." Dawn leaned forward and looked Isaac directly in the eyes. "Never trust a looking glass."

Isaac stepped back.

"The next test will be the scariest thing any of you have ever faced." Dawn matched Isaac's step and took his hands in hers. "I love you so much. Don't look into the mirror!"

"Isaac!" Lexie yelled.

Isaac opened his eyes, and he was lying on the ground of the tunnel. Lexie was standing over him with obvious concern on her face.

"I'm sorry," he said as he scrambled to his feet. "I'm awake!"

"Where were you?" Lexie asked. "I have been trying to wake you up for ten minutes. That wasn't a normal dream. You went somewhere."

Sweyn was standing on a rock beside Lexie.

"She's right," he said. "My magic couldn't even bring you back."

"I was with Mom," he said, still disoriented. "I was in your house, in your room, and she warned me."

"Warned you about what?" Lexie pressed.

"She said not to trust mirrors. She said we were being tested. I don't know," he replied, shaking his head. "It's all so hazy and bizarre. Is this what you have been dealing with? It's confusing and awful."

"Welcome to my world," Lexie said with a small laugh.

"We should get moving." Isaac sighed. "I'm not sure what we're walking into, but I want to get through it."

"Agreed," said Lexie.

"Interesting choice of words, child. If you check your map I think you'll find the way out of the tunnel has presented itself," Sweyn said as he lowered himself down from his post. "I believe that is what your mother was trying to warn you about."

Isaac and Lexie both looked deeper into the tunnel, following Sweyn's gaze.

"No," Isaac whispered.

"What is that?" Lexie asked as she took a step forward, looking past her brother.

"It's a mirror," Isaac responded solemnly.

Where once the tunnel had seemed to go on indefinitely, a mirror now stood gleaming in the light of their fire. Slowly, Lexie pulled up her arm and let her bracelet fall down to her wrist.

"Show us," she whispered as the now familiar light of the Anauz sprang into action. The beam shot out directly into the heart of the giant mirror.

"That's strange," Isaac said as he started moving down the tunnel.

"What is?" Lexie asked while following his steps.

"The light from the Anauz doesn't reflect off the mirror. It passes straight through," he responded, coming to a halt just a few feet from the mirror.

"You'll note, child"—Sweyn said as he landed on Isaac's shoulder—"it doesn't reflect us either."

Lexie lowered her arm, and the light from the Anauz disappeared into itself as she stepped up to her brother's side.

"Does that mean we can pass through as well?" she asked.

"It's more than that, child," Sweyn responded. The concern on his face deepening. "I've heard of this mirror magic in the past. It is dark; it is twisted; it is not of the fairies, and it is always a trap. Once you get inside, the only way out is to find the right mirror to the right world. It does everything it can to trick you. It distorts reality until you can no longer tell what's real and what's just a demented reflection of reality. If I thought there were any other way to Cain, I would never cross over that threshold."

"You keep saying 'it'. You mean, the mirror?" Isaac asked, still staring into the reflection of the cave.

Sweyn stifled a small laugh., "No, child, I mean the Keeper of Reflections. It's not often a doorway opens to the Keeper's domain. It will do everything it can to make you stay. But keep in mind the Keeper can't see anything for what it truly is. It's curse is a backward world devoid of light and truth. Be mindful of every step you take."

Lexie took a step forward and placed her hand up to the mirror.

"Let's do this together. Whatever happens on the other side, we never lose sight of each other, and we don't stop moving until we're through."

"Agreed," said Isaac as he stepped up beside his sister. They met each other's gaze for a moment, and Isaac could see the worry on Lexie's face. "We can do this."

Lexie nodded in agreement and turned back to the mirror.

"Mom says, 'Sometimes fear doesn't go away, always do what has to be done, even if you have to do it afraid.' Do you think she was just preparing me for this?"

"I think everything she's done and everything she's said, every story and every piece of advice, was to prepare you for this place. Now let's show her it worked."

Isaac took Lexie's hand, and together, they stepped through the mirror and into a world of complete darkness and unknown chaos.

Lexie lifted her arm, and without a word, the Anauz sprang into action, creating a calm blue light that washed over everything around them, bringing their new world into focus.

"What is this?" Lexie gasped as she stepped closer to her brother.

"It's the opposite of everything you know," Sweyn said, still perched on Isaac's shoulder. "We're inside the mirror."

The trio found themselves standing in an inverted version of what had been Lexie's first bedroom. It was a place she hadn't seen in years. It was a room that existed now only as a vague memory of a time before the moving started, before the Blanket Man, before the fear and nightmares. This was her happiest place or, at least, a reflection of it.

"This my old room," Lexie whispered. Slowly, she let go of Isaac's hand and began to wander around the space. "This is all wrong!" she said as she spun around, suddenly overwhelmed with irritation. "The bed should be over there. The walls were a light blue, not red! There were no mirrors in here, just my princess posters!"

Isaac looked around. On each wall, mirrors were scattered about hanging haphazardly. Cautiously, he stepped up to the closest one; in it, he could see his own reflection. His mother's words echoed inside his head, *When you look into the mirror, what do you see?*

He stepped closer, looking past his reflection to the room around him. It didn't seem right either. Even in the reflection, everything seemed out of place. The walls were even darker, and he realized Sweyn and Lexie weren't there.

"Isaac," Lexie said with a quiver in her voice, "back up."

Isaac turned and looked at his sister. Fear washed over her, but she wasn't staring at him; she was looking past him at the mirror. He turned back and immediately saw the problem. His reflection wasn't moving with him. He was there, staring back, but his movements didn't match. Isaac took a step back while maintaining eye contact with himself, but the reflection didn't budge. Instead, a slow menacing smile began to spread across his reflections face. Terror swept over Isaac.

"Never trust a looking glass." A voice echoed softly behind them.

The children spun around. The wall behind them had become a series of mirrors; a dark reflection shifted from place to place like a storm cloud caught in the wind.

"Isn't that what your mother told you, boy?" the voice said with a chuckle. "Moms know best."

"Are you saying we shouldn't trust you?" Lexie asked.

"I'm not a mirror!" the voice whispered sharply in her ear as the dark cloud surrounded them.

"You're the Keeper," Sweyn said as he lifted up off Isaac's shoulder. "We ask that you allow us to pass. We have business with the Queen."

The Keeper's laughed echoed all around them.

"So formal, little fairy. I appreciate your request. However, if the Queen were interested in your business, she would not have sent you to me. No, the rules will remain the same. If you want out, you'll have to find the way like everyone else. I don't play favorites."

"What are the rules?" Isaac asked, following the shifting mist with his eyes.

"Oh, the rules are simple." The Keeper laughed. "Stay sane while searching for each other, and just maybe, you'll find a way out. Fail, and you stay here with me."

"What do you mean, 'find each other'? We're all right here," Lexie asked.

"You're very astute." The Keeper chortled, "That will serve you well."

The dark cloud filled the room and began to thicken. Lexie turned quickly and reached out for Isaac, but she couldn't see anything. The little bit of light they had was muted by the ever-growing cloud. The children began to cough as the air seemed to be sucked out of their lungs.

Gasping, the trio fell to the floor as the voice around them rang out. "When you look into the mirror, what do you see?"

# CHAPTER 9

# The Queen's Castle: Level 4
# Lexie and Isaac (Continued)

*I see things that no one should*
*I see things you never could*
*I see the fire; I see the sea*
*I see it all inside of me*

*Lexie*

When Lexie opened her eyes again, she was standing in a long hallway lined with mirrors of every size and shape—some with small simple wooden frames and others with large ornate, almost gaudy, enclosures. Slowly, she began to make her way forward, carefully calculating every step.

Much like the cavern Cain was being held in, a radiant light danced up from the corners of the floor and walls. Like water, it moved in waves over everything it touched. This light washed everything in an unsettling red hue that made the hair on the back of Lexie's neck stand up. She could feel an uncontrollable rage building inside her. The constant movement made Lexie's stomach turn, and her head began to spin. She quickly reached out and grabbed for a

69

frame so she could get her balance. This was the first time she had looked into one of her surrounding mirrors.

Her eyes widened with wonder. Instead of the reflection she expected, she could see the vast expanse of the universe. Stars and planets swirling and spiraling in every direction. The beauty overtook her as a comet went streaking past her line of sight. It made her feel so small and yet, so very grateful. It was a magical thing to behold.

She took a step back and looked to the next mirror. In it was a woman, sitting on the edge of her bed, crying. Lexie stepped closer; she wanted to comfort her. The woman looked up, and for a moment, Lexie thought she could see her. With tears streaming down her face, the woman rose from the bed and walked up to the mirror. She stood there for a long time, having a conversation with herself. Lexie wished she could hear. After a few minutes of deep debate, Lexie watched the woman wipe her tears away, touch up her makeup, and with one final long sigh, walked out of the room to face whatever she had been preparing herself for.

Lexie moved on down the hall, still holding on to the frames for support. Each step caused her stomach to turn. It was difficult to keep her bearings; the hallway seemed to be never ending. After several minutes of torture, with little progress, she lowered herself down to the ground. She tucked her head in between her knees and closed her eyes. She had to calm her stomach if she was ever going to find her way out. Consciously, she controlled and slowed her breath, forcing herself to focus on the sound and relax.

"Feeling better?" the Keeper's voice asked.

Lexie jumped at the sound and slowly opened her eyes. The dark cloud they had encountered when they first passed through the mirror in the tunnel was floating low to the ground through the entire hallway. Grabbing the closest frame she could reach, Lexie pulled herself to her feet.

"Where are you?" she screamed.

"I'm right here," the voice responded as the fog surrounding her began to rise and fall, keeping time with her own breath.

"Where are Isaac and Sweyn?" she asked.

"That's not how the game works. I can't give you the answers. You have to do this on your own. Succeed or fail, it's you who decides. I am simply your humble host," the Keeper answered.

Frustrated, Lexie began to make her way further down the hall, glancing into mirrors as she passed. In most, she would see scenes inside people's homes—a family sitting down to dinner, a girl brushing her hair, a boy learning to shave—but it seemed that every few mirrors Lexie would catch her own reflection, some of the mirrors reflected in instead of out. Each time she saw herself, something seemed to be off. Her hair was the wrong color, the movements didn't quite match, the scene in the background would be different. She didn't understand, but she wasn't planning on stopping to investigate.

With her stomach still turning, she tried to pick up the pace, moving through what she began to fear was a never-ending hallway. The fog that surrounded her made it impossible to see her own feet or the floor beneath them. A small panic began to move its way up her spine. Lexie could hear her heart pounding faster and harder inside her ears. Every instinct inside her was screaming for her to run. She took off.

But as suddenly as her sprint began, it ended. Lexie tripped over a wooden frame on the floor, hidden by the fog. She fell hard. And for a few moments, she simply lay there with her eyes closed, trying to catch her breath and silently assess if the pain in her ankle and creeping up her arms was anything to worry about. Slowly, she opened her eyes and let out startled scream.

Throwing herself back and rising out of the fog, she yelled at the top of her lungs. "What is that?"

The Keeper's laugh was deep and eerie as the fog around her began to swirl and part, revealing the mirror onto which she had just fallen.

"When you look into the mirror, what do you see?" his voice whispered.

Lexie eased her way forward on her hands and knees. Carefully, she positioned herself on top of the mirror. With her heart racing and her body trembling, she looked deep inside, and there, staring back, she saw herself—only, a dark twisted version. The face was the same, the hair was the same, but the eyes, large dark black orbs, peered back at her through the mirror.

Lexie stifled a gasp as a slow smile spread across the mirror version's face, revealing razor sharp teeth, each filed to a point. She tried to lift herself up, to move away from the mirror, but the fog that surrounded her was now on top of her, making it almost impossible to move. Lexie fought against the pressure, but the more she resisted, the more pressure she felt on her back. She was being pushed toward the mirror.

"What's wrong, little girl. You don't like the portrait I've painted of you?" The Keeper laughed as the reflection began to sway back and forth, moving with the rise and fall of the dark cloud that surrounded them both.

"That isn't me," Lexie whispered, shaking her head.

"Oh, but it is," the Keeper whispered back. "There's a darkness inside you, truly reflected. It is beautiful."

"No," Lexie said as the Anauz on her wrist began to glow. The fog around her grew thicker, heavier, making more difficult to breathe.

"You can't deny your darkness. Embrace it. Let it free." The Keeper growled.

Lexie smiled. "My mom always said, 'There's nothing in the darkness that isn't in the light,' I finally understand what she meant."

Meeting the gaze of her contorted reflection, Lexie raised her right hand off the wooden frame and, slowly, lowered it to the mirror surface.

"I may carry darkness, but I serve the light," she said with resolve.

As her hand met that of her counterpart, the blue light of the Anauz swept over her, covering her head like a helmet. The light pushed past the mirror and swept over the reflection. Lexie's alternate closed her eyes and threw her head back, letting out a primal scream as the light covered her. Slowly, she lowered her head and opened her eyes. Lexie smiled—as did her reflection—now a true version of herself. The light of the Anauz pulled back into itself and remained just a soft glow under Lexie's sleeve.

"What have you done? The Keeper sneered. The dark cloud containing him that filled the hallway began to swirl and contract, finally settling in the shape of a large imposing shadow just a few yards in front of her.

Lexie scrambled to her feet.

"You cannot trick me, Keeper, and you cannot scare me," she nearly screamed.

With every other word, she took another step toward the shadow as the light of the bracelet began to increase, surrounding her with its glow.

"You are an obstacle that stands between me and my little brother. I will not be stopped. I will not be silenced." A fire flashed in Lexie's eyes. "Elymas cannot have him!"

The shadow of the Keeper stepped backward, avoiding the light emanating from Lexie.

"The sorcerer is who sent you here? You, poor little girl. You don't stand a chance," he hissed.

"No," she said as the light around her grew brighter. "You don't."

*Isaac*

Isaac opened his eyes and slowly lifted himself up off the ground. His head was spinning, and his heart was racing. He took a moment to try to calm himself down while he took in his new surroundings.

He was in a short hallway; the walls were lined with mirrors that reached from floor to ceiling and were only separated by a few cracks here and there. A sickly yellow glow emanated from the cracks in the walls and floor.

Isaac took a step forward, and the mirrors around him sprang to life. He looked to his right, and he could see himself as a small child, walking through a park, holding his mother's hand. He watched as his younger self stopped to pick a wildflower and hand it to his mother who smiled from ear to ear and bent down to kiss him on his forehead.

A tear rolled down Isaac's cheek as he turned away and looked into the mirror on his left. He saw Lexie and Cain, sitting on the family room floor in a fort they had built out of sheets and pillows. They were laughing and talking as a reflection of himself crawled into the fort with them. He could see the joy in his eyes as his little brother threw a small pillow at his reflection. They were so happy. There was so much love and joy in this scene; Isaac's heart sank. These were things he had never known—things he would never know.

"You can go there," the Keeper said.

Isaac jumped back, startled by the sound. The dark cloud of the Keeper had settled along the floor like a thick fog.

"What do you mean?" he asked in a voice that seemed too small for the moment.

"That could be you, sitting on the floor with your brother and sister. You could go to the park with your mother. You can be with your family. Just step through the mirror, and it's all yours," the Keeper said reassuringly.

"Step through the mirror? But these things you're showing me aren't real," Isaac said as he looked back through the mirror. He could all but hear his sister's laugh as he watched Cain and his reflection wrestle inside the fort. "They can't be."

"It's as real as you want it to be. Anything you could hope for, anything you could want, is waiting for you." The Keeper laughed. "Just step through the mirror. Away from the light, you can claim the life you've always wanted. Claim your family. You don't have to be a soldier in a cause you didn't choose. Here, you can be together with your family, forever."

A smile spread across Isaac's face as he watched the scene play out and start over again, like a video placed on loop. Slowly, he stepped back from the mirror and faced the cloud that surrounded him.

"The offer is very tempting, old fairy, but you have made one small mistake in your assumptions."

"And what is that?" The Keeper sneered.

"That there was ever a moment I wasn't with my family," Isaac said, tears still welled in his eyes. "I have been there every day. I am with them, and they are with me. We are already together forever."

"You have made your choice then." The Keeper laughed. "Good. I would have been very disappointed if you had taken my offer. This...will be much more fun for me."

Isaac saw movement ahead of him at the end of the hallway where it split going left or right. Lexie was standing there, in the mirror, staring off into the distance. Isaac ran, making his way to her, but she couldn't seem to see him. She was talking to someone, but he couldn't see who. Slowly, she began to take steps backward. He could see the fear in her eyes. Tears were forming as she screamed at whatever was in front of her. Isaac pounded against the glass of the mirror, but it had no effect. She had no idea he was there. He yelled for her; she couldn't hear him.

Isaac stood helpless as he saw the object of her fear; the wolf from the sandstorm stepped out from the darkness. He watched as Lexie turned to run, and the wolf launched its attack against her, leaping on her back and biting at her neck. Isaac's heart dropped as he fell to his knees, watching an attack he could do nothing to stop.

The cloud of the Keeper surrounded him.

"Maybe that's what's really happening," he whispered in Isaac's ear. "Maybe this..."

The scene in the mirror changed. Lexie was climbing a rock face. Isaac's heart was beating inside his throat as he watched her carefully place herself with each hand and foothold. She was just a few feet from the top; he knew she could make it. In his head, he was cheering for her, trying to help her climb with sheer force of will.

With a sudden movement, she looked down into the ravine below, and Isaac could see the scream she let out, even though he couldn't hear her. His eyes widened in terror. Lexie pressed herself against the rock and closed her eyes. A dragon, larger than anything Isaac had ever seen, came barreling from the deep, headed straight for his sister.

Isaac quickly turned away. He couldn't watch, he couldn't see anything else hurt Lexie. Nearly defeated, he rose from the ground and took a few steps into the hall to his left. Every mirror sprang to life, each with a different scene containing his sister, each equally horrible.

"What is this?" Isaac growled as the rage inside him began to build.

"These are all things that could be happening." The Keeper laughed. "One of them actually is. The name of the game is 'save your precious sister.' Enter the right mirror. and you will be reunited. Enter the wrong mirror, and you will stay here with me, forever. A reflection for eternity."

Isaac found new hope in the Keeper's words. If there was a chance of being reunited with his sister, then she was still alive; he would find her. He took off down the hallway, quickly glancing from right to left assessing every scene that unfolded to determine if it was the right one. He saw Lexie facing monsters in every form: dragons, three-headed snakes, wolves, and giants. He watched as she stood and fell against storms of fire, water, and darkness. He stumbled over his own feet as he came to a sudden halt. Darkness—there was something different in this scene. A huge smile spread across his face as he watched his sister stand up to a dark shadow figure, easily twice her size. There was no fear in her. He could see the strength of her words as she took steps closer to the monster. He could see the light of the Anauz as it swept over her and radiated from her.

Isaac laughed at himself for a moment for being so weak.

"I thought I had to save her, that she couldn't stand on her own. That was my fear," he said aloud.

The revelation swept over him as he took a step closer to the mirror. Everything he had seen—each mirror wasn't a reflection of truth but a reflection of his own fears. His own mind had worked against him to create the terrors he had watched unfold.

"Perhaps, this is a fear as well"—the Keeper's voice echoed through the hall—"a fear that she doesn't need you after all."

Isaac smiled. "No. We will always be stronger together. Let me show you."

"No!" the Keeper called out, but it was too late. Isaac stepped through the mirror.

# CHAPTER 10

# The Queen's Castle: Level 4 Sweyn and Reunion (Continued)

*All of these things, your mirror will reveal*
*When you look past you to the you that is real*
*When you look into the mirror, what do you see?*
*When I look into the mirror, I see all that is me*

*Sweyn*

Sweyn opened his eyes. He was lying on the floor of a golden hexagonal enclosure. It reminded him of an ornate birdcage he had seen in the human world. It was beautiful for a prison. Each of the six sides contained a small round mirror directly in the center, like a porthole. Carefully, he sat up, taking in his surroundings.

He crawled to the edge, peering over the side. There was light beyond the cage that let him know he was in a much larger space. Its deep indigo glow washed over the stone walls surrounding him. He couldn't make out the floor through the thick dark fog that ebbed and flowed beneath him, like the sea during a storm.

Grasping onto the closest golden bar, he pulled himself up, being careful to avoid looking in any of the mirrors.

"Okay, cousin, what are the rules to your game? How do I get back to my companions?" he said, staring off into the distance.

"Simple game, simple rules. Look into the mirror." The Keeper's voice echoed.

"What will I see?" Sweyn asked.

"That's the fun of the game, old friend. I don't actually know." The Keeper laughed. "For some, the mirrors may reveal the secrets of the universe, for others a way out of my game, but for most, they simply reveal the inner self. Be it anger or fear or pain…My mirrors are windows to true reflection. Now, look into the mirror."

Sweyn stepped up to the closest mirror and braced himself. He didn't know what to expect, but he was determined to do whatever he had to, face whatever horrors, to be reunited with the children. With trepidation, he peered through the first mirror, and what he saw broke his heart.

Cain was lying in the center of the cube Lexie had described. He watched as the Elemental weaved its way in circles around the child, occasionally whipping its tail against the glass, making Cain jump and curl tighter into a ball. As a tear ran down Cain's cheek, Sweyn's eyes also welled up. He stepped back from the mirror and shook his head in disgust.

"What kind of creature takes pleasure in torturing a child?" he asked as he moved to the next mirror.

The Keeper remained silent, content to observe the events as they were unfolding.

In the second mirror, he watched as the small boy sifted through piles of rocks, setting aside the most beautiful ones.

"Diamonds," Sweyn whispered to himself as he smiled.

It was a sunny summer afternoon, and Cain and his sister were building a fairy circle in their yard. Cain was carrying a handful of stones to leave as gifts when he tripped over a root in the ground and scraped his knee. He cried out as his sister came running. Sweyn stepped closer to the mirror, wishing he could reach in and comfort the child.

In the third mirror, Sweyn watched as Lexie stood in a long red hallway of mirrors, screaming into the darkness. He could see the anger on her face, the purest rage. She took off running, as fast as she could, but it was all for naught. There was no end to her prison. No escape. His heart raced as she dropped to the floor, her rage transforming into defeat as she accepted her fate.

With a heavy heart, he moved to the fourth mirror. Washed in a jaundiced yellow light, Isaac was pounding on the glass of a mirror. Sweyn could see the fear in his eyes; whatever he was seeing was the stuff of his own nightmares. The pain in Sweyn's chest grew as Isaac slid to the ground. The tears pouring from Isaac's eyes weren't for himself but for whatever it was he had just seen. Isaac closed his eyes and leaned his head against the glass. He was done.

Heartbroken, Sweyn moved to the fifth mirror and looked inside. He could see Dawn sitting on the porch of her house. She was holding a photo of Lexie and Cain when they were small, and the tears were streaming down her face. He could see a slew of activity around her—lights flashing, people running back and forth, dogs combing the ground. But Dawn was doing nothing. Sweyn looked deeper into the mirror, and he saw the darkness surround her. Worse than that, she accepted it. He watched as the last flickers of hope left her eyes.

Nearly defeated, he moved to the sixth and final mirror. It showed the beautiful landscapes of Fairyland; he could see his home. The light was shining bright, and the fairies were bustling about as they do on any day. Sweyn let out a gasp and grabbed ahold of the sides of the mirror as he watched darkness sweep through the land. He saw the terror on his friends faces as they rushed into their homes, trying to hide from the waves of evil washing through the village. All that was once covered in light and beauty was now a barren wasteland.

"That's enough," Sweyn said as he stepped back from the mirror. "I don't know what you're trying to do here, old monster, but I won't be a part of it any longer."

The Keeper chuckled. "I'm not doing anything. The mirrors choose what they reveal."

The Keeper's laugh turned into a sneer. "In you, they show… compassion." He hissed. "It's sickening. You are so much more than these pathetic children, and yet, you feel sorry for them. You want to help them. You can't stand to see them in pain. You are weak! And your weakness is why you will stay here. You lose the game."

"No, friend. The game isn't over. What you consider my weakness is my greatest strength," Sweyn said as a smile flickered on his face making its way to his eyes. "You see, I know these children. I can feel their pain, their anger, their fear, their love, their hope, and their resolve. I know what you have shown me here is a farce, tiny bits of truth sprinkled into a pot of lies. I find the pretense irritating, and your blatant mockery of their true character infuriating. You dwell in a world that can't possibly understand them. You are trapped in darkness. They are light. And I, old fairy, can feel that light. You haven't won them, and you haven't won me. More than that, you haven't even trapped me."

At that, Sweyn disappeared.

*Reunited*

Lexie took a step closer to the Keeper; Isaac stepped out of the mirror to her left and took his place at her side; Sweyn appeared from thin air, hovering at eye level to her right. Together, they faced down their host.

"We've won. We've beaten your game," Lexie said as her light grew even brighter. "Release us. Send us back so we can save our brother."

"You haven't won anything, little girl. If the sorcerer has him, your brother's fate is sealed." The Keeper barked, but the strength in his voice was wavering. "You may have seen through my mirrors, but your true selves have been revealed. You will never be anything more than an angry little girl, a scared little boy, and a weak old fairy. You may be together, but that means nothing more than a coalition of frailty. Your little brother won't survive Fairyland, and you won't survive each other."

"Despite your best efforts, you couldn't keep us apart," Isaac said. "Your words are that of desperation."

Sweyn spoke up. "Everything you have shown us has been a lie. Everything you say is a lie."

"It's funny to me how fine the line between lies and truth can be." The Keeper sighed. "You're together now, and that's great, but your resolve means nothing."

"It means everything," Lexie said. "We each were so fixated on the individual lies you told us, we missed the greatest truth."

"And what is that?" the Keeper asked as his shadow began to fade.

"You have no power beyond what we have given you." Lexie's eyes closed as the words left her mouth.

The light of the Anauz swept through the entire corridor.

One by one, the mirrors lining the walls began to crack and shatter. Each small explosion sent glass flying through the air. As the light surrounded the shadow, cracks began to appear in its form where the fragmented mirrors pierced. The Keeper let out a deafening howl as it shattered along with its entire domain, the force of which knocked the trio to the ground. The brightness of the light increased in a sudden blinding wave that just as quickly receded back into the bracelet.

The mirror world was destroyed.

# CHAPTER 11

# The Queen's Castle: Level 5

*I believed my heart so cold, harder than stone*
*And I feared if I let it go, I'd be left here, alone*
*It came to me so long ago, when I was but a child*
*I let it grow inside of me; I let my hate run wild*

As their eyes adjusted to the low light, a new landscape came into focus. Lexie assumed when they broke out of the mirror, they would be back in the same tunnel where they entered, but this was very different. The trio stared on in a mix of wonder and terror at what they now faced.

They were at the very end of the tunnel. A few feet in front of them, it opened to a vast cavern; if it had a top or a bottom, they couldn't see it. With calculated steps, the children approached the edge of the tunnel. In the distance, there was a low hum and a buzz of electricity. Lexie and Isaac leaned out of the mouth of the tunnel. In front of them was a sheer drop into the dark abyss. Lexie raised her arm and held the bracelet out. The light rolled out like a wave over sand, quickly finding the only available path—a small catwalk along the rock face to their left. It was no more than a foot wide and jaggedly uneven. Both kids stepped back.

"Any thoughts?" Lexie asked as she let out a long sigh.

Isaac and Sweyn both simply shrugged.

"Any chance you want to scout ahead, see what we're walking into?" Isaac asked, staring at the fairy.

"None at all, child, but thank you for asking," he responded with a smile. "Whatever we're headed for, I think its best we face it together."

"I think you're right," Isaac said, stepping closer to edge. "Whatever is making that sound seems to be getting louder."

Lexie stepped up beside her brother and eased past him onto the catwalk, keeping her back against the rock face.

"Have I mentioned that I don't care for heights?" she asked.

"Only once or twice, child," Sweyn said as he flew out to her side. "And, as before, I'll be right here by your side."

Isaac moved out onto the walkway beside his sister. As he did, a large stone door came crashing down behind him, sealing the tunnel they had just left.

"Looks like we're committed now," he said with a laugh.

Lexie let out a laugh as well.

"You know, a week ago, any one of the things we have faced down here would've given me nightmares for a month. Now, I feel silly for ever being afraid."

"That's how all of life works, child," Sweyn said, keeping pace with the children as they slid along the stone wall. "It never gets easier. You just grow stronger. There isn't less to fear. You just grow braver."

*Well, he's half right.* A voice echoed inside their minds. *There isn't less to fear.*

"Elymas!" Lexie screamed as she turned to her brother.

*Let's see how brave you really are*, the sorcerer's voice whispered.

The hum in the darkness grew louder, and bolts of electricity began to shoot out of the darkness below them. Each strike against the rock face creating a deafening boom and sending stone flying through the air. A wind came sweeping through the cavern; it carried with it sounds, like people screaming. As it hit the travelers, Sweyn was swept away. Isaac tried to catch him, but he was too late. Lexie threw her arm out, and the light of the Anauz shot out like a rope, grabbing Sweyn by the waist and pulling him back to his companions. Isaac reached out and grabbed ahold of Lexie's outstretched arm just as boulder fell directly behind him, destroying the path. The light of the Anauz wrapped around Isaac and Lexie's waists, binding the three together.

"We have to keep moving!" Isaac shouted over the howl of the wind.

Lexie nodded and turned back to the path ahead, but as she went to take a step forward, a bolt of electricity struck the wall, creating a rock slide that demolished the walkway. Lexie's heart felt like it was going to beat out of her chest. The wind was blowing so hard she could barely see past the dust and debris.

She turned back to the others and yelled over the sounds of despair that surrounded them, "I don't know what to do. I can't see the path."

"Do you know what's more powerful than a bitter old sorcerer, child?" Sweyn called out over the raging wind. "Everything. Including a small wood fairy."

Sweyn pulled back from the other two to give himself more room. Isaac and Lexie stared at him in disbelief. Before their eyes, he began to shift and transform, turning into a beautiful and giant harpy eagle. He was easily three times larger than an actual bird and equally as fierce. His long black-and-white feathers stretched out, allowing him to catch the wind blowing across the canyon. The light of the Anauz was still wrapped around his waist as he caught the wind that lifted him further into the air. He looked down at the children, and they could see the light was also burning in his eyes. With a mighty flap of his wings, the wind carried him even higher, lifting Isaac and Lexie from the crumbling walkway and into the darkness.

Sweyn caught another wave of wind and went even higher. He could see the electricity in the cavern below continuing to crash into the stone walls. Each boom left more of the footpath they were on destroyed. He looked on ahead of them. Even with his new sight, he couldn't see where they were headed, but the hum they had been able to hear since they left the mirror realm seemed to be growing louder. It gave him a destination. Even if he couldn't see where he was going, even with his path completely obscured by darkness, he knew he could get them there as long as he listened.

"Do you think he can see where we're going?" Lexie called to her brother. Even though they were dangling just a few inches apart, the sound of the wind rushing past their ears obscured almost everything else, save the occasional flash and boom beneath them.

"I hope so!" Isaac laughed back in response.

In the distance, Sweyn could finally see something coming into view—a small light flickering. He adjusted his course and began his decent toward the light. The mechanical hum they were headed toward was deafening as they made their approach. Lexie and Isaac held on to the light like a lifeline as they swooped down to a large stone platform where two torches burned bright, highlighting a large metal door, similar to that which they had first passed through at the beginning of their journey.

Sweyn began to bat his powerful wings, slowly lowering the children down to safety. As their feet touched the stone, the deafening mechanical hum stopped, leaving the children's ears ringing loudly in their heads, and the light of the Anauz pulled back into itself. Only the torch light remained to guide them. Once Sweyn was sure the children were safe, he wrapped his large wings around himself and, with a flip in the air, transformed back into his fairy self.

"So," Lexie said, staring at Sweyn, "you could've done that at any time? You could have turned into a bird and just carried us through?"

Sweyn smiled as he perched himself on a large boulder near the edge of the platform.

"Not just a bird, child. I can take the form of all manner of creatures. I'm a fairy of the woodlands. Rabbits, squirrels, foxes, and crows are my most common forms when I'm out and about in your world. They're naturally rather skittish creatures. I would say, more than half of the animals you have encountered were probably fairies just making their way through. It does take a great deal of energy and effort to maintain a form. I'm not sure I'll be able to do it again for a while. Even as a rhino, I'm not sure I could get us through that door. Besides," he said, flying over to the metal barricade for a closer look, "what would you learn if you had someone carrying you through every obstacle you faced in life?"

Lexie and Isaac followed Sweyn to the door, and she placed her hand on the surface. She expected the Anauz to light up and do its thing like before, but nothing happened.

"It isn't doing anything," she said as she curled her hand into a fist and banged it against the metal.

Isaac stepped up beside his sister. "You know the bracelet is just a conduit, right? It doesn't react to situations. It reacts to you. If it isn't opening the door, then some part of you must think there's another way through."

"That's insane," she replied, "I don't know which way to go. I never have."

"But you do," Isaac said with a smirk. "Every time you lift your arm and the light comes out, it's you. You carry the light inside you, like I carry it inside me."

"So why am I here, if you could have done all this without me?" The irritation in her voice was obvious.

"We all have our own purpose, our own talents, our own skills. None of us could have made it through this place alone." Isaac lifted one of the torches out of its sconce and turned back to his sister. "So, which way?"

Lexie picked up the other torch and looked around the stone platform. Aside from the door and a few boulders, there was nothing else around. She walked back to face the metal barricade, and as she did, her mind wandered to her little brother. She could see him, sitting in the center of his prison, tears streaming down his face as the creature he called the Elemental circled his enclosure; Cain's whole body jerking as the monster slapped his tail against the side. The thought was all she needed; her resolve was restored as the light of the Anauz began to pulse against her wrist. She lifted her arm once more and placed her hand gently on the center of the door.

A smile spread across Isaac's face as he watched his sister embrace her inner light. He could see the strength of her love for Cain and the power it commanded.

Sweyn flew over and landed on Isaac's shoulder, "I've seen all manner of magic, child. The good and the bad. I've been around a very, very long time, and I have never seen the likes of this. You children aren't fairies, but you aren't quite human either. This is the oldest magic, the purest. What are you that you can wield it?"

Before Isaac could answer, the door began to creak and moan as the metal expanded and contracted from Lexie's touch. Splinters of metal flew out as huge cracks shot through the door. Lexie closed her eyes and pushed slightly forward with her palm. It was a small action, but it was all it took. The obstacle came crashing down in front of them. What was once a large door, seemingly impenetrable, was now a heap of twisted and broken metal.

The mechanical hum came back with a vengeance; the sound wave nearly knocking the trio to the ground as they looked through the doorway into the unknown. The wind in the cavern behind them began to rage once more, and the crash and boom of electricity filled the air with the prickles of static.

"What is that?" Lexie shouted to her companions.

"Some sort of machine," Isaac screamed back. "We have to shut it down!"

Inside the newly revealed room, an enormous metallic structure stood in absolute contrast to the organic world around it. It was another stone room, much like those they had passed through already, but vastly larger. The machine itself looked like something out of a science fiction movie; an eerie orange light poured out of it in every angle. The travelers could see gears spinning, large tanks emptying and refilling, and electricity arcing between massive magnets. The majesty of the engineering it took to create such a monstrosity was a sight to behold.

As they made their way down a narrow stone staircase along the rock wall, toward the base of the edifice, Lexie could see cables running out of the machine and into the stone walls. Isaac tapped on her shoulder and pointed toward what looked like a small door leading inside the mechanism. Lexie nodded, and they carefully crossed the stone floor to the doorway. Isaac used all of his strength to wedge the door open with his body. If they were making any noise, it was completely obscured by the sound of the tumultuous structure they now stood inside.

Isaac and Lexie both had to stoop down to walk through the small metal hallway; it was definitely created for someone much smaller than them. The orange light that surrounded the building also radiated inside, adding to the inorganic nature of the place. The hallway had no doors, save for one, at the very end. The light that poured through the cracks around the door pulsed along with the resonate mechanical hum. Lexie led the way down the corridor, her head pounding from the noise. She could feel it through her whole body, each wave of light and noise resounding in her bones.

Very carefully, she approached the small wooden door. It was ornately engraved with a beautiful tree in full bloom. Lexie reached out and ran her hand across the leaves. When she did, it was like a swift wind blew through the scene on the door; the branches on the tree waved, and leaves fell to the ground. A smell of spring flowers filled the hall. It was a much-needed reminder of the beauty outside and the magic that surrounded them. Lexie turned to her companions, and her joy shifted quickly to terror; they were gone.

Darkness stood in place of the hall she had entered. She quickly turned back to face the door but instead of the engraving, she now stood in front of a massive towering tree. The hum she had begun to grow accustomed to was now replaced with the high-pitched whistle in both ears that slowly faded out to silence.

# CHAPTER 12

# The Woods: Part 3

*You stand there and listen staring right into my eyes*
*Your face begins to glisten in the pale morning sunrise*
*I see the light surround you I hide from its rays*
*I run back to the darkness to remain all of my days*

Lexie stood up straight. She was no longer in the hallway. Slowly, she took in her new environment. She was back in the woods but not a place she knew. Everything around her was washed in the low light of dusk; wherever this was, it was going to be very dark soon.

She took a step back and looked at the tree. It was exactly like the one carved in the door, so beautiful. A light wind blew through the branches, causing the leaves to rustle and release a sweet scent that put a huge smile on Lexie's face. She couldn't deny how happy this place made her. Anywhere was better than where she had been. She closed her eyes, lifted her face to the sky, and took in a deep relaxing breath. She liked it here.

In her mind, she knew she needed to get moving, but the longer she stood there, the harder it was for her to remember why. Carefully, she lowered herself to the ground and leaned back against the tree. She watched as fireflies began to rise from the ground; the flashing of their lights lulling her even further into a trance-like state. She felt very at home here. Why was she so worried before? She couldn't remember. She sat up quickly; her mind racing. What was she doing?

She was going somewhere. Where? She had been looking for something. What was it? Her heart was pounding in her chest; she was forgetting something important.

Another wave of wind blew the scent of wildflowers toward her. Whatever it was, it couldn't have been that important. She sat back against the tree, and every muscle in her body relaxed.

*Do you know where you are?* A familiar voice echoed in her mind.

Lexie smiled as she said, "I'm in a happy place."

*Do you know who I am or why you are here?* the voice asked.

Lexie searched her mind for the answers. She knew this. Her heart began to speed up again as the gentle breeze washed over her. She relaxed further into the tree and smiled.

"No."

*Good, and you are right. This is a very happy place. Now go to sleep and rest for a while. It will all be over soon.* The voice reassured her.

"Lexie!" a new voice screamed.

Her eyes shot open. The roots of the tree had started to grow over her legs, holding her to the ground. She tried to struggle free, but the roots were now wrapped around her stomach. Another wave of sweet-smelling air rushed over her, but this time, she was prepared. The Anauz sprang to life covering her from head to toe with a force field of light, blocking out the poisonous pollen that had been filling her lungs and clouding her mind.

*There is no need to struggle, sweet girl,* the voice whispered in her mind. *Take a calming breath and relax.*

Lexie stopped her battle with the tree roots. The harder she fought, the tighter they squeezed. It was getting difficult to breathe. The roots tore into the skin of her wrists. Carefully, she searched the trees around her, looking for any sign of her silent captor.

"Where are you, old friend?" she asked. Her mind now completely clear, and her purpose restored.

*Ah, so you do remember me?* Elymas laughed as he stepped into her line of sight.

"How could I forget you for any length of time?" Lexie asked in a hushed tone. "Your voice is as familiar to me as my own thoughts."

Elymas stepped closer to his captive. *How is it my magic never seems to work on you?*

"Maybe you're losing your edge, sorcerer," Lexie whispered.

*What are you doing?* Elymas's voice echoed loudly in Lexie's mind as he took a hesitant step backward. *Oh, you are a clever little girl, aren't you?*

"I have noticed a few things over our encounters," Lexie said, her voice barely audible. The light of the Anauz that encompassed her began to grow brighter and radiate out. The roots that held her down struggled to maintain their grip, but the power of the light was too much. They released their hold and disappeared back into the ground.

"First, your power is based solely on fear." The light lifted her up and held her in the air so that she was at eye level with her captor. "And I am not afraid of you."

Elymas took another step back. The world around him was shaking, and even the ground felt unstable beneath his feet. His heart began to race as Lexie matched his movements.

"Second"—Lexie smiled as she moved within feet of her tormentor and softly said—"you don't react well to the power of my voice."

*You will never make it to your brother!* Elymas sneered.

"Guess again!" Lexie shouted.

The full force of her voice hit Elymas like a tank, knocking him back into the darkness of the woods and the safety it provided him. He scrambled to his feet and, as quickly as he had appeared, he was gone again.

*You may be clever,* his voice murmured in her mind, *"but you haven't won."*

"Yet," Lexie said as the light lowered her to the ground and pulled back in to a soft glow around her body. "But I'm about to."

The world around melted away, and she was back hunched over in the hallway from which she had been taken. The door with the ornate engraving was wide open, and on the other side, she could see Isaac and Sweyn moving silently along a metal catwalk which surrounded a large and sickly-looking Ash Tree. The metallic tentacles that she saw outside running into the rock face were also in here, connected to the tree, and the same orange light illuminated the entire central chamber.

Lexie stepped out onto the catwalk and peered over the railing. She was three stories from the bottom and another two from the top. The enormous tree filled the entire space; its long limbs reaching out and touching the metal grating of the walkway wherever it could. On each level, different size cables connected with the tree. Lexie turned her attention back to her companions. They were on the opposite side of the chamber and were heading for a ladder which connected the multiple levels of the structure. She tried to get their attention, but the droning hum of whatever was at work here muted her every attempt.

Determined to catch up, she took a step forward and prepared to run when the deafening noise suddenly stopped. An eerie silence fell over the chamber. Lexie froze in place and looked to her brother. He had turned away from the ladder and was looking at the tree. She waved her arms wildly trying to get his attention.

"Isaac!" she yelled.

As the word left her mouth, the entire complex sprang to life. A dozen doors on each level that she hadn't noticed shot open simultaneously, and the chamber filled with fairies of all shapes and sizes bustling around seemingly unaware of her presence. She watched as some fairies stopped to inspect the leaves and branches of the tree, while others monitored the extensive cables and connections going to and from the trunk. Carefully, she moved along the railing toward Isaac and Sweyn who were still frozen in place beside the ladder with their backs pressed hard against the wall.

As she slid along the rail, one of the small offshoots of a branch grazed her arm, and she let out an excruciating scream. The pain she felt in that moment was more than she had ever experienced in her life. She closed her eyes and fell to her knees. It took her a few moments to catch her breath as the pain of the encounter wore off.

Still trembling, Lexie opened her eyes. All the creatures around her had stopped in place and were staring at her. Terrified and slightly embarrassed, she rose to her feet. No one moved. No one spoke. She searched the faces of everyone in front of her, looking for some hint of emotion. Were they angry? Did they realize she wasn't supposed to be there? Finally, one of the smaller and older-looking fairies broke the stagnancy and flew up to meet Lexie's gaze. His grey hair hung shaggily around his face, and his long beard matched it in both color and need of a trim.

"I am Baldr the Dryad, Chief Keeper of the First Tree," he said, staring deeply into her eyes. "What are you that you can survive its touch?"

"I'm Lexie. I'm just a girl," Lexie responded softly.

Baldr smiled, and his eyes twinkled.

"You're not 'just' anything, little one. Even with all the magic we command, this Tree remains beyond our grasp. It was cursed a very long time ago with the darkest of magic. It greedily absorbs energy from all it touches, and its roots run very deep in our world and in yours. To touch it is almost certainly to die. You are only the second I have seen survive it."

Lexie looked around; everyone was still staring at her. Isaac and Sweyn had silently made their way along the wall and were standing just a few feet away.

"What is this place?" she asked.

"A very long time ago, we didn't need to create energy. The sunlight gave us everything we could need or even want, but now, the further the Queen moves underground, the more power we need to create to keep things in order. The Tree is very old and very strong. It serves the Queen as a generator," Baldr answered, while still searching Lexie's face. "There is something familiar about you."

Lexie met his gaze and smiled. "I just have one of those faces." She turned and looked at the tree, and her smile faded. "It's in pain."

Baldr furrowed his brow. "And why do you say that?"

"When I touched its leaves, the pain I felt wasn't my own. This Tree is in agony." Lexie reached out her hand to touch the Tree's leaves a second time.

Baldr quickly zipped over and blocked her hand.

"Are you insane, child! I just told you, you were lucky to have survived the first encounter. A second will definitely kill you. That is the curse, a constant need for more energy, a bloodlust that can never be quenched."

"Can't you break the curse?" Lexie asked as tears welled up in her eyes.

Baldr looked even deeper into Lexie's eyes. "No, I can't. This is an ancient magic. Only a few still exist who can harness such power."

A smile spread across his face, and his eyes lit up as he looked past Lexie and saw Isaac and Sweyn still pressed firmly against the far wall.

"How strange it is, after saying that, to see there are two in this room with the Power of Light."

A wave of excitement washed over everyone in the building. Isaac and Sweyn made their way across the platform to Lexie. The air was thick with electricity as Isaac stepped to his sister's side. Baldr tried a few times to silence the crowds, but with no luck.

Sweyn looked around the room and saw the chaos that was growing. He landed on Lexie's shoulder and whispered in her ear, "You and your brother are the only ones who can break the curse placed on this Tree. Darkness cannot reign in the presence of Light."

Lexie looked at Sweyn and knew what had to be done. Her eyes moved to Isaac, and he nodded. Together, they stepped closer to the Tree.

"What are you going to do?" Baldr asked.

"The curse is that of greed," Isaac replied, "placed by forces of Darkness. A gift freely given by servants of Light will destroy it."

"What will you give?" a voice called out from the background.

Isaac and Lexie took each other's hand, and together, they reached for a low-hanging branch.

"Everything," Lexie whispered.

The light of the Anauz rushed out and covered the children, quickly turning from the familiar blue to a blinding white. The closer they got to the Tree, the brighter the light burned. As they placed their hands on the branch, it wasn't the children who cried out, as most of the fairies expected, but the Tree.

A horrible high-pitched screech filled the air as the ground beneath them began to rumble and shake. Outside of the Castle, all through Fairyland, and into the human world where the roots of the Tree had grown strong, the ground shook, and the cries of the Tree could be heard.

Dawn stood on the porch of her house, staring out into the darkness of the woods that surrounded her. A tear ran down her cheek as the cry reached her. The bustle of people who were rushing back and forth looking for Lexie and Cain all froze as the ground trembled. Alex ran to the porch and looked up at Dawn.

"What is that?" he yelled over the screams.

"It's a tree," she whispered as she slowly lowered herself down on the deck. "The children have made it to the Tree."

Out of the darkness of the woods, two small beacons of light appeared. Dawn stood up and quickly began to make her way toward them. Alex followed her to the tree line and watched as she carefully stepped across the barrier.

"Where are you going?" he asked, terrified she was losing her mind.

Dawn stopped in her tracks as the two lights came to rest in front of her. "It's time to go back," she whispered.

"Time to go back where?" he yelled. "Dawn, where are you going?"

Turning her head only slightly, she calmly replied, "I'm going to Fairyland to get our children. It's almost over."

With that, she reached out and touched the lights, disappearing, just as Lexie had.

Lexie and Isaac slowly drew their hands away from the Tree. The light of the Anauz pulled back, but instead of returning to the bracelet, it surrounded the children with a soft glow, giving them an other-worldly look as they turned back to the crowd of fairies.

Behind them, the once diminished and drained ancient Tree rose to its former glory. Completely restored, leaves began to bloom, and the withered branches now stretched out, placing pressure on the walls of its prison. The trunk of the Tree nearly doubled in size, sending the cables which had been attached to it flying in every direction.

"Everybody, out!" Baldr yelled. "She's going to take the whole place down!"

Creatures took off running, flying, and slithering in every direction.

Lexie looked to Sweyn. "Where do we go?" she yelled.

"Follow me, child!" he called back as he took off.

The children had to run to keep up with up Sweyn as he led them down the passages they had used to enter the building. They burst through the first small door they had entered just as the Tree broke through the top of the structure. The metal edifice which housed the Tree crumbled like an aluminum can under the expansion of branches. The trio stopped just in front of the crowd of fairies that had gathered to watch the scene unfold.

The once eerie orange glow had been replaced with a bright green light which seemed to radiate from each leaf. Grass, moss, and flowers sprang up in every corner of the chamber, covering the stone floor and walls in the life which it had been denied for so long. When the Tree finally ended its unfurling, the entire chamber was as beautiful as the world outside the Castle.

Baldr flew up to Lexie and Isaac.

"Thank you," he said with tears in his eyes. "We have lived in the darkness for so long, I had all but forgotten what was lost."

Lexie smiled. As beautiful as this place was, she knew they couldn't spend any more time.

"Protect the Tree. We have to save our brother."

Baldr nodded and backed away, motioning toward a passage on the far end of the chamber.

"The path to the Queen. Be careful," he warned as he turned his attention to Sweyn. "Watch over them, cousin. They are the hope we did not know we had given up."

Together, the companions made their way across the chamber and stepped through the opening and into the darkness of the passage. The light which surrounded Lexie and Isaac receded into them as the glow of the Tree dissipated. Isaac lifted his hand, and a flame sprang forth, offering generous light. Little did they know, this was indicative of what was still to come.

# CHAPTER 13

# The Queen's Castle: Level 6

*There's a fire in your eyes*
*Burning hotter than hell*
*There's an evil in your eyes*
*Like an angel who fell*

Isaac lead the trio down the now all-too-familiar stone passage to an end they couldn't see. Lexie couldn't fight the sick feeling which was growing inside the pit of her stomach. Every instinct inside her head was telling her to turn and run. Whatever dangers lay ahead of her, her brain did not want her to face them.

She quickly ran through possible scenarios that could be on the other side of the passage. She didn't know how much further it was to Cain, or even if he was still in the glass prison. What if they had taken him somewhere else? What if they had hurt him? What if there was no end to this ridiculous tunnel? Lexie shook her head, trying to get her mind to calm down and focus on where she was. She had been so lost in thought, she hadn't even noticed she was starting to sweat, or that the once smooth stone floor had become uneven and treacherous.

"That light of yours would be awfully handy if this were an ice cave, child," Sweyn said with a chuckle as a bead of sweat ran down his forehead.

Isaac stopped and turned back to face his companions. Lexie could see the hesitation in his eyes. His clothes were soaked completely through, and his hair was matted against his head. Something was wrong.

"What is it?" she asked as she wiped her brow with her sleeve.

"It isn't me," Isaac answered.

"What do you mean, child?" Sweyn asked as he landed on Lexie's shoulder.

"My fire is just light," Isaac said, holding his hand out so the others could reach the flame he carried. "There is no heat to it. It isn't real fire. Something else is happening here."

Lexie reached out and touched the flame that flickered in Isaac's hand. She smiled as she passed her hand through it without burning.

"He's right. It's the same temperature as the air."

Before she could pull her hand back, a howl came echoing through the passage. The sound wave bounced off the walls, and the ground beneath them trembled. Small fissures appeared in the surrounding rock as the tunnel filled with dust. Another howl rang out, and the stone floor splintered like split wood. As the cracks began to spread, gases from below started to creep into the air.

"What is that smell?" Lexie cried out as she tried to cover her face. The air was choking her, and her eyes felt like they were on fire.

"Brimstone," Sweyn said solemnly.

"What? Lexie coughed.

"That's a little melodramatic, fairy." Isaac laughed, causing him to cough even harder. "It's sulfur. We must be near a lava flow."

"Lava?" Lexie laughed through her coughing. "Of course, we're in a volcano. Why wouldn't that be a thing?"

"We have to get out of here This air isn't getting any easier to breathe," Isaac said as he turned back to continue down the passage.

A third howl came barreling down the tunnel and hit the travelers with a powerful blast that knocked all three of them to the ground. The cracks in the floor and walls began to separate rock from rock, turning into huge gaps and dividing the children. Lexie and Isaac both struggled to regain their footing.

"You have to jump!" Isaac yelled as the gap between them widened.

Sweyn flew up and hovered over the gap. "Jump now, child, before it gets any further!"

Lexie took a few steps back from the edge of the void and prepared to leap.

"Wait!" Isaac yelled, stopping his sister midstep and causing her to fall forward.

Sweyn zipped down and grabbed her by the collar of her shirt, pulling her back from the edge just as boiling hot lava filled the breaches in the floor. Lexie looked up to thank Sweyn but gasped as she watched the ceiling of the passage disappear. The walls then dissolved into the liquid rock that surrounded them, revealing a vast lava field filled with dark, black solid rock and flowing streams of glowing ooze in every direction.

"Another trap," Sweyn said. "A very clever one, we brought ourselves here." He flew up high into the air but couldn't make out any clear path to take. Shaking his head, he lowered back down to Lexie.

"I have lived a very long time, and I have seen all manner of things. I sat idly by while my world began to twist and turn, and I said it didn't affect me. I chose not to know. I chose not to care. But I see now what that decision has caused. This is my fault," he said as he settled on the ground by Lexie's feet. "Fairyland used to be a place of beauty, a place of peace. It was a paradise."

Lexie lowered herself down and sat in front of him.

"You didn't do this," she said reassuringly.

"Worse than that, child. I allowed it. Me and my kind, we were supposed to take care of Fairyland. We are it's stewards, and we have failed." Sweyn dropped his head, and Lexie could see the shame.

"This isn't over. Fairyland still exists. There is an evil that has invaded, but it hasn't conquered. It can't win unless we give up, and we will not give up." Lexie rose to her feet. "We are going to save my brother, we are going to restore your paradise, and we are going to send Elymas back to the darkness."

Lexie lifted her arm, and the Anauz slipped out from under her sleeve.

"Which way?" she asked, but the bracelet did nothing. She shook her arm out and lifted it again. "Which way?"

Nothing.

Isaac let out a laugh. He had been silently watching and listening from the other side of the lava stream. Lexie turned to him, her irritation flashing in her eyes.

"Something funny over there?" she yelled. "The bracelet is broken!"

"You don't need the bracelet. I've said it a few times, but you still don't seem to get it. So yeah, that's funny. Forget the Anauz. It served its purpose. The power is in you." Isaac chuckled.

Lexie took the bracelet off and slipped it into her pocket.

"All right," she whispered under her breath, "which way?"

A blinding white light shot out of her in every direction, knocking Sweyn over and forcing him to cover his face. Lexie turned in a slow circle and looked at the area through the sight the light was giving her; she could see further than should have been possible. She felt so warm and safe. The light grew even brighter as she embraced it.

Isaac smiled as the light wrapped around him. "Finally," he said to himself.

"There!" Lexie said, pointing out in front of her. "There's something that way."

Sweyn forced himself up off the ground, still trying to block the light with his arm. He took a few steps forward and peered into the abyss.

"Ha!" He let out a hearty laugh. "The boy is still leading us. It's a diamond!"

The light slowly dimmed as it pulled back into Lexie. Her sight remained fixed on the white stone ahead of them. Everything seemed so clear now, like she had been seeing this world through a fog that was suddenly cleared. Isaac took a few steps back from the edge of the lava flow and, without hesitation, took a running leap, landing only inches on the other side of the now four-foot gap. Lexie reached out and grabbed his arm as his feet hit, keeping him from stumbling backward.

"Thanks!" he said as he regained his balance and stepped up beside his sister. "You see where we're headed?"

"I do," she said as she turned and looked at her brother for the first time with her new sight. She gasped. She could see the light radiating from him like a beacon. "What happened to you?"

Isaac laughed. "Nothing at all. You are just seeing me for the first time through open eyes."

"Is this how you see things?" she asked. "Is that how I look to you?"

"Now it is," he replied with a smile. "I could always see the light in you, but it was guarded. Like you were keeping it locked away. It's free now, and it burns bright. Our bridge is nearly complete."

"I don't know what you two are going on about," Sweyn chimed in as he flew up and landed on Isaac's shoulder. "You both look exactly the same, just...happier. Which you shouldn't. Things are about to get really bad."

"Why do you say that?" Lexie asked, looking down at the little fairy.

"You know that big three-headed Elemental snake that's been guarding your little brother and the wolves that have been following us pretty much the whole time we've been here?" He asked.

"Yeah," she said as a cold chill ran down her spine.

He leaned forward and whispered, "They're in here with us."

Both children went into a defensive posture as they quickly scanned the horizon looking for the threat.

"There!" Lexie yelled, pointing off to the left of their position. "Wolves."

"And there," Isaac added. "The Elemental. It can go into the lava!"

He watched as the monster slithered across a stone portion of the lava field and then disappeared into an active flowing river of molten rock.

"Then it can be anywhere," Sweyn said as he lifted up off Isaac's shoulder and looked anxiously around them.

"The wolves are just watching us. What do we do?" Lexie asked. "I think they're trying to figure out how to get to us."

"The plan hasn't changed. We need to follow the stones and get out of here. If the Elemental is here, then we have to be close to Cain. We need to hurry," Isaac said.

"We can't just run. There are a dozen lava flows standing between us and the diamond, and who knows how many more past that. Some of them are too wide to jump." Lexie looked at Sweyn. "Any chance you can turn into a giant flying wombat or something and carry us out of here?"

"I can't, child. I've been trying to change since the walls disappeared. I don't have the strength. And even if I did, a giant flying wombat?" Sweyn laughed despite the situation and shook his head. "That would be a sight to behold, I suppose."

Lexie stepped up to the edge of a large gap in the rock and turned to her brother. The light emanating from her doubled in magnitude as she smiled.

"What are you going to do?" he asked.

"I'm thinking, leap of faith," she said.

Isaac laughed. "All right. 'Leap of faith' into the lava or 'leap of faith' across the giant no-way-you'll-make-it river of doom?" he asked sarcastically.

Lexie smiled wide, but before she could answer, the Elemental came bursting out of the molten river in front of her. Isaac threw himself forward to catch her before she hit the stone floor, breaking her fall. Together, the children scrambled backward as the giant snake came crashing down on the stone in front of them, its three heads moving back and forth while its forked tongues flicked through the air. Steam rose steadily off its body as it slithered closer to them.

All three heads pulled back at once, preparing to strike, only to be stopped by a long and harrowing howl that came pouring forth from the wolves. With the Elemental distracted, Lexie and Isaac both clamored to their feet.

"What do we do?" Lexie whispered to her brother. "There's nowhere to run."

"We do what we came here to do. We fight," he said with resolve.

The Elemental turned its attention back to Isaac and Lexie. Lexie could feel the power of the light surging through her. She straightened her arm by her side a sword of burning white light appeared. Isaac smiled at his sister as a sword appeared in each of his hands.

The giant snake reared back its heads and hissed at the children. With a quick flick of its tail, the monster lunged forward, attacking with all three heads at once. Lexie dove under the far-right head as a ball of fire came pouring out of its mouth. She rolled under its powerful neck and, with one swift slice, removed its head from its body.

At the same time, Isaac leaped forward. Before the other two heads could even react, he drove his swords up through the bottom of their powerful jaws, piercing the brain. He pulled his swords out and spun around, quickly removing the heads in one fell swoop.

As the lifeless body of the Elemental slipped back into the river, the lava began to harden, and the gaps started to close.

"We have to run, now," Isaac said.

"Why? Soon we'll be able to just walk across the gaps," Lexie said.

"So will the wolves," Isaac said solemnly.

Lexie turned and looked at the wolves in the distance. They were pacing impatiently along the edge of a large lava flow.

"You're right, they'll be able to cross soon."

"Come on, children!" Sweyn yelled from the distance. Lexie turned and saw he was waiting near the white stone Cain had left behind. "They're coming!"

Lexie and Isaac turned just in time to see the lava solidify enough for the wolves to hop across and take off toward them.

"Run!" Lexie screamed as she grabbed Isaac's hand and took off. Together, they leaped from the first ledge and into the still active lava flow. The light wrapped around them, and when their feet hit the still molten rock, it became instantly solid, allowing them to run straight across the stony field without being burned. Sweyn flew up into the air and watched as the wolves struggled to cross where the lava still lazily eased by.

"Stay with us!" Isaac called.

"We can see the path," Lexie added.

Sweyn flew down and struggled to meet the children's pace as they raced through the lava field and into the unseen. As more and more of the lava hardened, the light in the chamber dissipated, but for the first time, Lexie was completely unaffected. She could see everything in front her with a clarity she had never known. Sweyn pushed himself and managed to grab ahold of Isaac's shirt.

"Hold on tight!" Isaac yelled. "We're going straight through!"

Sweyn clenched his fists around Isaac's shirt and closed his eyes tight. He had no idea what they were going straight through, but there was no way he was letting go. Lexie glanced at her brother as they approached a giant silent waterfall; he didn't bat an eye as they drew closer.

"Hold your breath and jump!" he yelled as he dove head first through the wall of water.

Lexie took a deep breath, closed her eyes, and dove behind him.

# CHAPTER 14

# The Woods: Part 4

*So you give up and fall into its arms*
*The darkness embraces you; you fall subject to its charms*
*When from the distance, comes a light*
*It starts off dim and then gets bright*

For a few moments, Lexie remained still. The ground she landed on was soft and welcoming. The sound of rushing water surrounded her, and she could feel warm sunshine on her face. She didn't want to open her eyes. If this was a dream, she wanted to stay in it as long as she could.

"Lexie?" Isaac whispered. "Are you all right?"

Slowly, she opened her eyes. She was lying next to a beautiful waterfall on a mossy knoll. Isaac was leaning over her with a very concerned look on his face.

"I'm fine," she finally answered as she pulled herself upright. "Where are we?"

"I have no idea," he said as he looked around. "There's something familiar about it though. I don't think we're in the castle anymore."

Lexie stood up and took in her surroundings. After a moment, she lit up.

"I know exactly where we are! I haven't been here in years, but this is the waterfall close to my grandparent's house! Mom brought me here when we first moved in. She said she spent a lot of time here when she was little."

"Where's Sweyn?" Isaac asked.

Lexie looked around. She hadn't realized he was gone. "He came through the waterfall with you, didn't he?"

Before Isaac could answer, there was a rustle of leaves behind him and the sound of muted voices.

"Someone's coming," he whispered.

The children jumped over a large fallen tree and ducked behind its trunk. Lexie lowered herself all the way to the ground and looked through a narrow split between the tree and the earth. Isaac carefully peeked around the base of the trunk and waited for the voices to get close enough to see. He couldn't quite make out what they were saying, but the tone was that of concern, maybe even fear.

Lexie held her breath as two beings stepped through the trees and into focus. They stopped just before the stream leading out of the waterfall and faced each other. One was a girl, maybe sixteen or seventeen years old. She was tall and thin; her long brown hair in a side braid over her shoulder. She was wearing light-blue jeans and a familiar zippered sweatshirt. The other was a man, easily a foot taller than the girl, dressed all in white, with long blond hair tied at the base of his neck with a brown leather strap, and he carried a large horn over his shoulder. He was other-worldly. The light Lexie could see when she looked at her brother was also radiating from inside both of them.

The man was obviously saying something to the girl she didn't want to hear. He was speaking vehemently and making wide gestures with his long arms. The girl planted her feet and crossed her arms, shaking her head the entire time. Lexie knew that stance. She knew that furrowed brow and disapproving stare. She had been on the receiving end of it more than once. She smiled as she watched the interaction between the man and her teenage mother.

Lexie reached up and tugged on Isaac's sleeve. He turned and looked down at her.

"That's our mom," she whispered. "We're in the past."

Isaac's smile matched his sister's. "Time is relative," he whispered back. "The past for us is the present for her. It's all happening at once. She's talking to a Paladin."

"I know," Lexie said as she rose to her feet, shifting her gaze to her mother. "She told me this story."

Dawn and the Paladin fell silent as their attention turned to Lexie, who was now standing in full view. Isaac waited for a moment then stood up and moved to his sister's side. Together, they climbed over the downed tree and walked to the opposing edge of the stream.

"Lexie," Dawn said with a smile as she looked at her daughter. "You look exactly the same as the last time I saw you, though your light seems to burn brighter. That was seven years ago."

"Only hours for me." Lexie reached over and grabbed Isaac's shirt sleeve, pulling him closer to the stream. "This is your son, Isaac."

"It is wonderful to meet you!" she said as her heart skipped a beat, and her eyes welled up with tears.

She looked up at the man with whom she had been speaking. His expression remained stoic, but there was a pain in his eyes he couldn't mask. Lexie could see it clearly when his gaze met Isaac's. There was a knowing there, something painful, which neither of them seemed willing to share.

"What is it?" Dawn asked, obviously picking up on the same tension as Lexie.

"How are you here?" he asked, never breaking eye contact with Isaac and ignoring Dawn's question.

"They have come from Fairyland," Dawn said with a smile. "This is Tyr."

"A Paladin," Lexie said as she smiled from ear to ear. "You used to tell me stories...or I guess, one day, you will tell me stories. 'He and his people protect us from evil while remaining hidden from human eyes.' I love those stories." She let out a hearty laugh. "I always thought you made them up."

"How are you here?" Tyr asked again. The seriousness of his voice never wavering.

"We came through the waterfall," Isaac said, matching the intensity in Tyr's voice. "We were in a deep level of the Fairy Queen's castle, being chased by giant wolves across a lava field, when the waterfall came into view. It saved us."

The joy on Dawn's face quickly turned to anger as she looked back at her daughter. For the first time, she noticed the tears in her clothing, the dirt covering her pants, the scratches and dried blood on her hands and arms.

"Why?" she asked, her voice shaking with rage.

"There is a sorcerer named Elymas," Lexie said. "He is an evil man who has poisoned the mind of the Queen."

Dawn tried to calm herself. "I know him."

"It gets worse," Lexie said, carefully judging her young mother's reactions. "We have another brother, named Cain. Elymas took him to the castle. We have been fighting to get him back."

"Why would you have to fight to get into the castle?" Dawn asked. "It is a place of peace."

"Elymas has poisoned the Queen's sight. She has moved the castle underground. She can no longer see the light," Isaac said, looking back and forth between his mother and Tyr. "The Fairyland you know now is not the Fairyland we have been fighting through. There are many levels, and all are filled with traps designed to keep the light out."

"No," Dawn said, shaking her head. She looked up at Tyr. "You can't allow this to happen!"

"We do not serve the fairies," he said. "They are responsible for their own land, for their own realm. Even if we wanted to help, we couldn't. We do not leave the light. Aside from that, the Queen's heart was already turning against men, otherwise, she would not have been so easily swayed."

Frustrated, Dawn turned her attention back to Isaac and Lexie. "Why would the sorcerer take my son?"

"I don't really know," Lexie said with tears in her eyes. "He has been there my whole life, just on the other side of the trees. Hiding in the shadows. Waiting for one of us to cross."

"I warned her not to trust him, and she cast me out." Rage flashed in Dawn's eyes as she turned back to Tyr. "We have to stop him!"

"You can't," Isaac said. Everyone turned to him. "You can't defeat him without us. The light that connects us keeps pulling us together, but we have to go back. We are so close to the center, so close to Cain. I can feel him, and he's terrified. Elymas draws his strength from darkness, from fear. He took Cain out of spite. He took your son to hurt you. He truly believes he has won."

"Why am I not with you?" Dawn asked. "The me of your time. Why would I let you go in alone?"

"The Queen cast you out of her land," Tyr said, looking down at Dawn. "You said the river bridge had been closed to you. It still is. The only way for you to get back in would be a new bridge, one that Elymas couldn't see, a bridge of light."

Dawn looked back across the stream to her children. She understood what Tyr was telling her, and it broke her heart.

"I'm so sorry that you have had to do this. I'm so sorry for the pain you have faced. I already love you so much! I promise I will do all that I can to prepare you for this."

"You did," Lexie said with a smile. "We have to go. We're running out of time."

Dawn started to step forward, but Tyr placed his hand on her shoulder. "You have to let them go."

He turned his attention to the children, making eye contact with Isaac. "Go to your brother," he said with a knowing smile. "Do what you were sent to do."

Isaac nodded and took Lexie's hand. "I love you, Mom. Remember that always."

A tear ran down Dawn's cheek as she watched her future children disappear, to face unknown darkness.

"What do we do now?" she said, still staring across the stream.

"We wait," Tyr whispered in response.

Lexie blinked and rubbed her eyes, trying to adjust to the sudden darkness as quickly as she could. Isaac grabbed her by her arm and pulled her down to the stony ground.

"Stay down," he whispered. "Something is here."

"Where are we?" Lexie whispered back.

She could feel a large boulder against her back, and the room they were in was so cold she was starting to shiver. She focused on the light she knew she carried inside her, and she immediately warmed up. Slowly, everything began to come into focus. There was a pinkish glow coming out of the cracks in the stone walls and floor.

"I'm not sure," Isaac said. He was slouched down beside her, his back pressed against the boulder. She could tell he was trying to adjust his sight as well.

"I'll tell you where you are, child." Sweyn's voice echoed out. "You're in my way. And after disappearing and leaving me all alone to face those nasty wolves."

"Sweyn!" the children said in unison.

"Where are you?" Lexie whispered.

With a small flash of light, Sweyn appeared as he had the first time they met him.

"Do you realize what I had to go through to get here?" he nearly yelled. "And just to find you already here having a little sit down!"

"We're sorry." Isaac laughed. "We didn't mean to disappear on you. It just kind of…happened."

"Oh yes, child, make your excuses," Sweyn said in a sarcastic tone. "Well, while you were diving through imaginary waterfalls, and I assume having a nice swim, then eating cake, and laughing about how you had left me behind, I had to get away from the wolves and find my way out of the chamber. No easy feat, mind you."

"We are sorry, Sweyn," Lexie said with a small smile still lingering on her face. "We didn't know we were going to disappear. We landed in the woods, in the past, with our mother and a Paladin."

"A Paladin!" Sweyn scoffed. "I'm sure that was a very magical moment for you. Did the giant blowhard have anything useful to say, or did he simply peacock around?"

"All he really said was that he couldn't help…" Lexie said reluctantly.

"Sounds about right," Sweyn said with a smirk. "Paladins never could be bothered with the affairs of fairies. Not that they should, child, but it would be nice if they tried."

Isaac smiled from ear to ear. "How did you make it out of the lava field?"

"Glad you asked, child. It's a fantastic story, but I'll save the details of my heroic escape for another time." Sweyn went on, "To keep it succinct, I disappeared as well, after you did. It was actually enjoyable watching those wolves look for me. They could smell me, but they couldn't find me. Not the brightest of beasts. I waited for a while until they gave up, then I went on.

"One by one, I found more of Cain's diamonds. Eventually, that led me to a passage out of the field and down a pitch-black tunnel. I couldn't see, child, so I opted not fly.

"On the ground, I stumbled over two more diamonds, letting me know I was still on the right path. After what seemed like an eternity, I could see light in the distance. I picked up the pace, knowing I was so close to the end. Starving, thirsty, exhausted, I emerged from the passage to see my two companions, that I was oh so worried about, mind you, just sitting having a chat."

Lexie and Isaac both let out another laugh. "We are so very sorry!"

Sweyn smiled. "Not your fault, children. I'd blame your mother if I cared to. Now, where are we?"

Sweyn flew up and peered over the boulder. Isaac and Lexie both turned and stood up to join him. Lexie's eyes widened as her heart skipped a beat then took off racing.

"Cain," she whispered.

"He looks frozen, child," Sweyn added.

"We have to get him out, now," Isaac said as he stepped back and made his way around the boulder.

Sweyn sat on Isaac's shoulder as he stepped onto the platform holding the glass cube. Lexie stood back and watched for a moment, waiting to see if anything was going to react to their presence. Nothing. Not a sound. Carefully, she moved forward joining her companions.

Inside the cube, Cain was lying on his side, curled up in a ball. Lexie could see the shallow, labored breaths he was taking. Her heart broke. She looked at Isaac and Sweyn. They were both desperately searching the outside of the cube for a way to get in. When she looked back at Cain, the light inside her couldn't be contained; it came pouring out. And as she placed her hand against the glass, it vanished.

Quickly, Lexie dropped down beside Cain and pulled him tight against her chest. His eyes were closed and lips and fingers were a bright blue. Tears streamed down her face as Isaac fell to his knees at their side. Sweyn stayed back and watched as the light came out of Isaac in a blinding wave, washing over him and covering Cain. The color returned to Cain's skin as he slowly blinked his eyes open. Lexie let out a laugh through her tears, and a smile spread across his face.

"You came back," he whispered.

"I told you I would," Lexie said as she held her brother tight.

# CHAPTER 15

# The Queen's Castle: Level 7 The Queen's Throne Room

*I know who you are, I know where you've been*
*I know everything about you, to your tiniest sin*
*I am the one who brought on your pain*
*I am the one driving you insane*

*A sweet reunion.* Elymas's voice echoed through their minds.

Lexie and Isaac scanned the room. There was no sign of him, no sign of anyone. Sweyn swooped down and landed on Cain's chest, carefully assessing his condition.

"It's going to be all right, child," he said to the small boy. "We are here to take you home."

"No," Cain whispered, "I can feel him. He's almost here. He won't let us go."

"He doesn't have a choice," Isaac said.

Cain shifted his gaze to his brother. "I know you."

"Yes," Isaac said with a smile.

The light which surrounded them all began to fade. Cain watched as the light receded into his chest, and a warmth washed over him.

"What is this?" he asked. "I can feel it inside me."

"It's a power that lives in us and protects us." Lexie reached into her pocket and pulled out the Anauz. "Here," she said, slipping the bangle onto Cain's arm. "This will help you control it."

Cain looked down at the bangle and watched in awe as it shrank down to fit his wrist and transformed from a shining metal bracelet to a thick brown leather gauntlet. Lexie looked up at Isaac, and he let out a small laugh.

"Everyone has their own style." He chuckled.

"I'm Sweyn, if anyone cares to know," the little fairy said.

Cain looked up to the fairy that was hovering a few feet in front of him. "There is something familiar about you too."

Sweyn began to speak, but before he could get a word out, the sorcerer's voice boomed in everyone's mind. *And I'm the Blanket Man.*

The three children scrambled to their feet, searching the darkness for any sign of the monster who had been tormenting them. Sweyn started to fly up, but an invisible force knocked him back down to the stone floor. The air became frigid and thin. Lexie and Cain began to shake from the cold; each breath they took created a small cloud of fog which dropped heavily and settled around their feet. The walls surrounding them fell away, revealing a vast chasm encompassed in darkness and disturbed only by the presence of a second platform in the distance, too far out to see what was on it.

Lexie stepped up to the edge of the platform, pushing Cain behind her. "This has gone far enough," she screamed into the abyss. "Let us go!"

*No need to shout,* Elymas's voice echoed through her mind. *I'm right here.*

The sorcerer appeared on the platform in front of Lexie. She stumbled backward, falling into Cain who was frozen in place. Isaac grabbed her before she hit the ground and helped her regain her balance. Isaac placed his hand on Cain's shoulder, and the Anauz on his wrist began to glow. Sweyn picked himself up off the ground and flew up to hover beside the children. Forming a small wall, the four stood against the sorcerer.

A smile spread across Elymas's eyeless face. *You think three children and an insignificant little fairy stand a chance against me?*

The platform beneath the children began to shake. They all grabbed for each other while they tried to keep their balance. A wind came swirling out of the chasm, carrying with it an enormous dragon. Lexie recognized it; it was the same dragon she had encountered on the beach, only something had changed. The dragon shot up into the air and then dove back down, flapping its enormous wings to hold its place behind Elymas. Lexie looked closer; the eyes were gone. On the beach, the dragon had her eyes. This dragon had none, yet she could feel it peering through her.

Before she could make any more observations or share any of her thoughts with her brothers, huge claws reached up from the darkness and dug into the stone floor. The children each took another step back as the large black wolf, which had been following them since the beginning of their journey, pulled itself up and stood beside Elymas. Lexie's breath caught in her throat. The wolf had easily doubled in size, and as it lowered its head and began a low growl, Lexie could see her own anger, her own hate, reflected back through its enormous eyes.

*Look at you, all of you, trembling with fear. You should have listened to me, Alexandria. You should have listened to my truth. You should have come with me when you were small. It would have saved everyone a whole lot of trouble.* Elymas stepped forward, his voice echoing in their minds. *Now I will offer all four of you to my Queen.*

"Four?" a familiar voice questioned from behind the children. "You may have miscounted."

The children and Sweyn all turned quickly to see who was talking. Lexie gasped, and a huge smile spread across Isaac's face. Dawn stood tall behind them, and at her side, stood Tyr. And behind them, filling the platform, was an entire assembly. Isola and Elmis stood at the head of an army of fairies and magical creatures.

"Mom!" Cain cried out as he ran into his mother's open arms.

"Hi, baby," Dawn said as she held her son tight. "Everything is going to be okay."

*How?* Elymas's voice sneered. *You were cast out. You cannot enter here.*

"You are a fool, sorcerer," Dawn said with smile. "You opened the door. You built a new bridge. You shouldn't have touched my children."

He cringed at the sound of her voice, but then, a slow smile spread eerily across Elymas's face.

*I had you cast out once, I can do it again*, his voice whispered in Dawn's mind.

The second platform, which had appeared in the distance, silently began to move toward the crowd. As it approached, an enormous throne came into view. Illuminated by an unseen force, it appeared to be made out of pure gold and covered in precious stones of all shapes and sizes. Out of the top of the throne, ten large golden horns jutted out and curled back, matching the seven on the head of the dragon. The steps leading to the seat were beautifully crafted bronze and iron with inset pearls and swirling opals. Lexie's eyes widened as she took in the beauty of the throne and the one who sat upon it. The Fairy Queen. Lexie had imagined this moment her entire life, but never had her mind been able to create anything this magical.

As the platform came to a stop, leaving a large chasm between the two, the Queen rose to her feet, revealing her full glory. She was the most beautiful creature Lexie had ever seen. Standing at least six feet tall, her frame was lean but strong, with alabaster skin, and long raven-black hair that fell in loose curls around her shoulders. Her eyes were like emeralds, and she wore a crown made of gold surrounded by sparkling red rubies which matched her lips. Her long sleeveless gown was as black as night, with small sparkles and swirls of colors. As she stood as still as stone, a small ball of light went streaking across her gown, and Lexie realized, it was a shooting star; the sparkles and swirls were the vastness of space.

The entire assembly was silent and still as the Queen's throne made its approach, but now, whispers and murmurs began to rise from the crowd as anticipation of what was to happen next grew. Elymas turned to face the Queen, and with a pure hatred burning in her eyes, the likes of which Lexie had never seen before, she gave the sorcerer a slight nod as she took her seat on her throne.

Elymas quickly turned back to the crowd and, with a smirk, transformed into a large and menacing eyeless white wolf. The wolf Lexie had seen throughout her journey, always in the distance, was now just a few feet in front of her. He and the black wolf both lowered their heads and began to growl. The dragon, which had been hovering, shot straight into the air and let out an ear-piercing screech. It circled the entire platform, breathing a constant stream of fire which surrounded the stone and filled the entire chasm with a river of flame. The entire chamber was now encompassed by the light of the fire, into which the dragon disappeared.

The two wolves both took a careful step forward but halted as Sweyn swooped down and landed on the platform in front of them, standing between them and the children. Elymas's laugh echoed through everyone's mind.

*Move, little fairy, before I gobble you up. It was a fool's errand to follow my prey. You should be very afraid.*

"You may not know me, sorcerer," he said as he stood his ground, "but I am neither a fool, nor am I afraid. We all have our role to play. Let me show you mine."

Sweyn flew a few feet straight into the air and, with a swift flip and a flash, transformed into a giant lion. Easily larger than the wolves, his golden mane seemed to shine from within, and his glassy eyes reflected the fire which threatened to engulf them. Elymas and the black wolf stepped back toward the edge, the fire licking at their tails, as Sweyn lifted his head to the sky and let out a thunderous roar. The stone platform shook, the ceiling of the cavern split, and the Queen shifted uneasily on her throne.

In a deep voice that matched the majesty of his new appearance Sweyn said, "Open your eyes, sorcerer, it has been too long since you have seen the light."

The Anauz pulsed against Cain's wrist as he left his mother's side and took his place beside his brother and sister. Together, the three were washed in the blinding white light they carried within them. Dawn and Tyr stepped forward as the light within them burst forth. Isola let out a beautiful laugh as the light washed over her and

Elmis and then spread like wildfire through the fairies and creatures that stood with them.

The dragon came screeching out of the depths of the fiery chasm, carrying with it an entire hoard of dark wolves and three-headed snakes which it dropped in the midst of the assembly. Elymas bowed his head then lunged at Sweyn who turned and met the attack head on. Behind them, a huge battle raged. With magic, swords, and vicious claws, light battled against the dark as the Fairy Queen silently watched from her throne.

Everything and everyone seemed to disappear as Lexie and the black wolf faced off for their final battle. Carefully, they circled each other, matching their moves. The wolf finally broke the standoff and attacked, baring its huge teeth as it leaped forward at Lexie's chest. She jumped backward, dodging the attack as the sword of light appeared in her hand. With a spin and a lunge, she swiftly sliced downward, removing the beast's head from its body. She could feel a weight lifted off her chest as the last spark of life remaining in the wolf's eyes faded away. Lexie finally understood what her young mother had meant when she said the wolves were them. It was her own anger, her own fear, embodied which she had just defeated. She looked up and saw the battle as it went on, but now, through new eyes. Every fairy and magical creature were being forced to face their own demons.

With renewed strength, she ran as fast as she could toward her little brother who was fighting a small Elemental with his bare hands. Isaac saw the same danger and began making his way through the onslaught to reach Cain.

The Elemental's three heads were attacking from different directions at once; Cain rolled and dodged each blow with calculated precision. He didn't fully understand the light that was surging through him, but he knew enough to let it have control. The more he surrendered to its power, the stronger and faster he became. The Elemental pulled back all three of its heads and readied for a final strike. A surge of heat and energy poured through Cain, and he couldn't help but thrust his arms out toward the creature. Lexie and Isaac both stopped in their tracks as they saw three daggers of pure white energy come shooting out of his hands, striking each head of the Elemental.

Without hesitation or fear, Cain turned and ran straight into the battle to join the fight.

Sweyn and Elymas fought on, matching each other blow for blow, bite for bite. Each strike more devastating than the last. The two were locked together, claws and teeth piercing the other's flesh as a surge of light built between the two of them knocking them apart with a small explosion. Both scrambled back to their feet as Dawn stepped in between them.

"Thank you, old friend," she said to Sweyn. "I can never repay you for everything you have done, but I can take it from here."

Sweyn bowed his head to Dawn and slowly limped away as she turned her attention to Elymas.

"I stood against you from the beginning, sorcerer, and now, I have returned to finish what I started so many years ago. The poison you have filled the Queen with will die with you."

Elymas's voice chuckled as it filled Dawn's mind. *You are as naïve now as you were when you were a child. I haven't poisoned the Queen. That was you and your kind. The hate and anger that drives all of mankind is what finally broke her. She saw that you didn't deserve the gifts you had been given. I was just there at the right time to fill a void man created.*

Dawn let out a small laugh as Isaac, Lexie, and Cain stepped up to her sides.

"There may be darkness in the world of men, but we serve the light, and it's time for you to face judgment for your crimes."

The light which covered them grew even brighter as Tyr stepped past them and toward the white wolf.

"The time has come, brother. You must go home."

Elymas could feel the heat of the fire behind him. He stumbled slightly as his heel slipped off the edge of the platform. Transforming back into his original form, he turned his head and smiled as he heard the wings of the dragon behind him.

*Not yet*, his voice whispered, and he quickly turned and leaped onto the back of the dragon as it passed by.

Dawn ran up to the edge of the platform, but it was too late; they were out of her reach. She quickly turned back and looked at

Tyr. She could see the pain in his eyes as he pulled a white bow and arrow from the quiver on his back.

"I'm sorry," he whispered as he let the arrow fly.

As it pierced the heart of the dragon, the beast let out a painful cry, reared its head back, and then fell. Dawn and her children watched as Elymas and the dragon disappeared into the river of fire.

Lexie turned back to the battlefield just in time to see the final wolf slain. Bodies and blood covered the platform, and a single tear ran down her cheek.

"It's over," she said with a sigh as the light which had surrounded them all began to fade.

"Not yet," Isaac said as he turned his attention to the Queen.

# CHAPTER 16

# Home

*I gave them all my word, they learned it through and through
But in the end, they turned away, there was nothing left to do
The choice is yours, and yours alone, what path that you should take
But keep in mind, through all of time, your soul has an eternal stake*

The Fairy Queen rose from the seat of her throne. Despite the distance, the rage in her eyes couldn't be hidden. With careful, graceful steps, she began to descend the stairs; each step closer to the bottom provided her with a new piece of armor. Her crown transformed into an ornate helmet. Golden gauntlets covered her hands and arms. A giant black sword, as reflective and radiant as glass, appeared in her right hand, and a matching shield in her left. As she took the final step onto the stone platform, her gown shifted from the beautiful majesty of the universe to pure fire. It wrapped around her like a river around a stone. The fury of which was reflected perfectly in her eyes.

"The only way to stop her is to cross the flames," Sweyn said. He had transformed back into his fairy self, and the wounds of his earlier battle were painfully clear. "I don't have the strength to transform again."

Tyr kneeled down and looked Sweyn in the eye. "You've done more than your fair share, small friend. Rest now," he said as he looked up at Isaac. "We knew it would come to this."

Dawn saw the exchange of looks between Tyr and Isaac, and her heart dropped into the pit of her stomach.

"No!" she yelled as she grabbed Isaac around his shoulders and pulled him in close. It was an embrace only a mother can give.

"No…" she whispered while her eyes filled up with tears.

"What is happening?" Lexie asked, her heart racing. She didn't understand the silent exchanges taking place, but she knew the look of heartbreak on her mother's face.

Cain took his sister's hand. "It's why he came," he said in that calm tone he used when he knew things no one else in the room seemed to realize. "To go where we can't go. To protect us. To protect you."

Lexie looked to Isaac who was still caught in his mother's arms. "No!"

Isaac gently pulled away from Dawn and took a step back.

"Cain is right," he said with a smile and wink to his little brother. "It's why I came."

"I can't lose you again," Dawn sobbed. "There has to be another way. I can go!"

"You never lost me," he said. His eyes welled up with tears. "I was always there, just out of reach."

Tyr stood up and placed his hand on Dawn's shoulder. He could feel the pain emanating from inside her.

"We serve the light," he said as if it justified what was about to happen.

Tears were streaming down her face as she looked up to her old friend.

"He's just a child," she pleaded.

A pained smile crossed Tyr's lips as he said, "You know he's not."

The light inside Isaac began to grow brighter.

He turned to Lexie. "You are so much stronger than you think you are. There is nothing in your world that you can't handle. I will always be with you. I am always in the light."

He looked down to Cain and smiled a huge smile as his light continued to increase. "Never deny the power inside you. You have gifts you haven't even began to use. Look out for our sister. Despite all of her strength, she has a tender heart."

"What are you going to do?" Sweyn asked as he struggled to his feet.

"I'm going to stand in the gap. I'm going to set the Queen free. I am going to do exactly what I came here to do," he said.

Isaac took a few steps back and looked to Dawn. She stood resilient as the light inside him began to shift his body and transform him into that of a full-grown man. Lexie and Cain gasped. He was tall and strong, dressed as a warrior. His long brown hair and bright eyes reminded Lexie of a painting she had once seen of a Norseman standing in a longboat.

"I have and will always love you," Isaac said to his mother.

With that, Isaac turned and faced the Queen who was pacing back and forth on the opposite side of the chasm. He took a moment to clear his mind. The light which encompassed him let out a blinding burst of energy, forcing everyone to cover their eyes. Isaac let out a hearty laugh and started walking forward.

Much like the Queen making her descent from her throne, pieces of armor began to appear on his body. His helmet was radiant silver, his sword and shield were made of pure white light. Each step closer to the edge made him even more fierce to behold. Dawn drew Lexie and Cain close against her as she watched Isaac step off the edge of the stone and walk gracefully across the river of fire.

"Mom," Lexie said with a voice so small and terrified.

"I know, baby," Dawn said with the reassurance of a parent. "He knows what he's doing."

A cracking sound drew everyone's attention to the top of the chamber. Where the stone had split, a large crack was spreading. Dust and debris fell onto the platform as a small beam of light broke through. Dawn smiled a knowing smile.

"That will do," she whispered.

Isaac stepped out of the river and onto the Queen's platform.

"Your Majesty," he said with a slight nod. "You have been dwelling in darkness for too long now. I have come in service of the light."

"There is no light here, young warrior," her angelic voice rang out. "You have caused a great deal of trouble for me just to save one little boy."

Isaac smiled. "I would have done it to save one, but no, I have come to save them all."

"Then let's begin." She sneered as she raised her sword and swept it toward Isaac.

Isaac deflected the blow with his shield and countered with a sweep of his sword. The Queen laughed as the fight ensued. Strike for strike, they each dodged and blocked, countering each other's moves with timed precision.

Lexie held her breath as she watched her brother battle the Queen. The suspense was too much for her as she took a step forward toward the fiery pit. Isaac glanced across the chasm at the movement, and it was all the Queen needed. She saw the small distraction and made her move, her sword slicing through his right side in one clean sweep. Isaac's dark red blood ran down his side in stark contrast to the glorious white he wore. Lexie screamed as her brother fell to his knees.

"You were a fool to face me alone. Your love for mankind is what makes you weak." The Queen smiled disparagingly.

"Love is the only true strength that exists, your highness." Isaac matched her smile as he rose back to his feet. "And I was never alone."

The Queen stumbled backward as she looked to the opposite platform. Dawn and Lexie both reached their arms straight into the air; a brilliant white light shot straight out of them like a laser. The crack expanded, and more and more light from the surface poured in. Cain raised his arms, and the small daggers of light began to shoot out of the Anauz, chipping away at the sides of the expanse.

"No," the Queen gasped. "Stop!"

"I'm sorry, your majesty, but you left us no choice," Isaac said as a host of warriors descended into the cavern, following the light and forming an entire army behind him.

"You were supposed to exist beyond light and dark." He began to make his way toward the Queen. "You were supposed to be a servant to mankind. They are an enduring and beautiful gift to this world. But instead, you chose darkness. You do not see the world as it is. You see the world through the blinders you have chosen for yourself. It will no longer be allowed."

The Queen dropped her sword and shield as she began to panic, facing Isaac and the horde of warriors that followed him.

"They made me this way," she pleaded. "They are the ones that are evil. How could I be expected to serve them when I am so much more than they will ever be? They are not a gift but a curse. How am I supposed to deny what I know in my heart to be true?"

"Your heart has been poisoned, highness. I will free you of that burden."

Isaac raised his sword, and in one smooth stroke, it passed through the Queen's chest and pierced her heart.

Isaac let go of the sword and stepped back as the Queen fell to her knees. The sword melded into her and was absorbed by her body as the flames of her dress overtook her. The fire raged, and the Queen let out a scream of excruciating pain as the flames shot out in every direction, completely engulfing and obscuring her form.

Lexie and Cain stood on the edge on their platform and watched in terror as the Queen disappeared in the flames. The screams quickly died down as the color of the flame shifted from its natural red-and-orange hue to a bright blue and then, ultimately, a blazing white. Isaac stepped toward the white flame and immediately retreated back, the heat singeing his skin.

"I am made anew." The Queen's voice echoed. "My heart is forged of finer steel."

Out of the white flame, the Queen emerged even more beautiful and radiant than before. Her crown was made of sparkling diamonds, and her long flowing gown was as white as freshly fallen snow. She stepped up to Isaac who was leaning heavily on his shield and clenching his side to try to stop the bleeding.

"Thank you for restoring me to myself. Your blood will not have been shed in vain. I will undo the damage I have allowed. Return home, warrior, there will be more battles for you to fight, but none against me."

The Queen reached into the folds of her dress and pulled out Isaac's sword.

Isaac carefully reached out, and the Queen placed the sword in his hand. A wind which was carried on the light that now filled the chamber swirled around Isaac and the army that stood with him. With mixed emotions, he looked at his family across the divide and shed a tear as he vanished into the wind, to return to the light.

The Queen stepped up to the edge of the platform. With a wave of her hand, the river of fire disappeared, and from the ashes, a beautiful garden emerged. What was left of the top of the chamber disappeared, and the warmth of the sun covered all that was once hidden from its glory. Flowers sprang up from the ground, and trees came into full bloom. As the Queen made her way toward Lexie and her companions, a warm wind swept through the valley, carrying birdsong and the spring-like hope of renewal that had so long been banished from the land.

"Your highness," Isola said, stepping forward. "It has been a while."

"Too long, sister." The Queen smiled as she turned to Dawn. "You have grown into a beautiful woman."

"Majesty"—Dawn said, motioning to Lexie and Cain—"allow me to introduce my children."

The Queen looked to Lexie and Cain, and her heart broke. "You carry the strength of your mother inside you. It's a family trait," she said with a wink.

"You are all welcome in this kingdom any time."

She turned and started to walk off and then paused. "Yes, even you, Paladin."

With a laugh, she transformed into a large white gyrfalcon and soared into the sky.

"Well, that answers a lot of questions I never cared to ask," Sweyn said, breaking the lingering silence.

"Same old Sweyn," Dawn said with a laugh. "I have truly missed you."

"What do we do now?" Cain asked.

Dawn looked down at her children, her heart rejoicing at their safe return and, simultaneously, breaking from the reopened wound of Isaac's absence.

"Now we go home."

After a few heartfelt goodbyes and promises of future visits, Dawn led her children out of Fairyland and back to the river crossing. She took each of them by the hand, and together, they walked through the water.

It was pitch black in the woods. Despite the light of his headlamp, Alex stumbled over roots and fallen trees. He could hear search dogs in the distance, and the radio he carried had constant chatter from the search parties keeping each other updated on their positions, when he heard the report he had been anxiously hoping for since the beginning.

"They're here!" a voice yelled over the radio. "They're all three here! I have them! They're okay. I'm leading them back to base."

Alex's heart skipped a beat as he took off running. When he finally reached the yard where a makeshift search-and-rescue station had been set up, he could see Dawn and the children standing there wrapped in dark heavy blankets, holding water bottles, and being questioned by the local police. He rushed over and scooped up his kids, holding them tight.

Dawn finished giving her statement to the police when something in the woods caught her eye. A flash of light that drew her in. Lexie and Cain saw it as well and stepped up on either side of their mother. All three smiled, and Dawn let out a sigh of relief as they saw its source—a man who would always watch over them, a warrior who would always protect them, a brother who would always guide them, and a son who would stand in the gap for them.

# POEMS TO INSPIRE A NOVEL

The Darkness

You stand there and listen
Staring right into my eyes
Your face begins to glisten
In the pale morning sunrise
I see the light surround you
I hide from its rays
I run back to the darkness
To remain all of my days

Missed Opportunities

I stand in the valley
I watch the coming flood
All around me, waters rise
Then I realize, it's their blood
On the hills all around me
On the mountains and the stream
Oh, Father God, I plea
Let this only be a dream
The children lay dying
Their blood on my hand
As I stand staring
At a godforsaken land
They look at me
Through tortured eyes
All they now hear

Are corruption and lies
I had a chance
To plant a seed
I had a chance
To help their needs
But I turned my back
I ignored their pain
Now the thought of their souls burning
Is driving me insane
I know I'm forgiven
And they're not forsaken
But deep in my heart
A large toll's been taken

The Tree

Colder than death
Darker than night
Both things describe
A heart full of spite
Living with anger
Breathing in hate
Not wanting life
Tempting every fate
Nothing seems precious
Nothing divine
Life is a waste
A waste of good time
Then suddenly
Up in the sky
A figure comes
From up on high
It swoops down to you
Lands at your feet
It stands before you
A demon you meet

You look into
Its deep evil eyes
Down inside you
Fear starts to rise
It reaches out
Clutches your hand
Suddenly, you're standing
In an unknown land
You look around
See nothing but a tree
Leaves, it has none
And of fruit, it is free
You're pulled to it
Tugged by evil desire
As you draw near
It's engrossed in fire
Above the limbs
A dark cloud grows
It moves toward you
Like a flock of crows
You cry out in fear
And leech to your host
But it can't protect you
From this unholy ghost
It passes right through you
Bearing piercing pain
You know if you stand here
You'll soon go insane
You fall to your knees
And cry to the Father
Your demon kneels before you
And says not to bother
It starts to tell you
Of things that have been
It can recall
Your every sin

It says the "father"
Would never redeem
A heart with such darkness
Bursting at the seam
So you give up
And fall into its arms
The darkness embraces you
You fall subject to its charms
When from the distance
Comes a light
It starts off dim
And then gets bright
From the light
A savior appears
As your demon
Cowers in fear
He reaches out
You grasp His hand
He takes you away
From this desolate land
You stand before your Father
And plea for your soul
Your heart breaks a thousand times
As the Spirit takes control
You think about the demon
Who held you by the tree
You think about your demon
Then you realize it was me

Don't Fall

It's ten past ten
And this room is growing cold
The candle's burning down
And the dark is getting bold
I see the sudden flashes of light

Hear the voices in the wall
They say so many things to me
But all I hear is "Don't Fall"
I know what they're talking about
I know exactly what they mean
And I know I should listen
For a burning future I have seen
It's more difficult than you'd guess
To give up one's true mate
I've been living here so long
Just me and my hate
I believed my heart so cold
Harder than stone
And I feared, if I let it go
I'd be left here, alone
It came to me so long ago
When I was but a child
I let it grow inside of me
I let my hate run wild
Years have passed, and here I lie
My demeanor bitter and sulking
But deep down inside of me
My heart of stone is broken
I'm not saying there's no hate
Or anger to recall
All I'm saying now
Is that never shall I fall

Eternal Stake

I've seen the pain
In their eyes
I watched them fall
Through great demise
I see them now
Though they are gone

Never again to see
A breaking dawn
I've seen their torment
And their pain
I'm certain that soon
I shall go insane
I heard them laughing
I saw them crying
I hear them screaming
I think I'm dying
Father, where am I?
Father, please!
I scream, and I shout
As I fall to my knees
Where are you now
And where have you been
How could one commit
Such unimaginable sin
A sin is just a sin
But their rejection was grand
I did all I could
To lend a helping hand
I gave them all my word
They learned it through and through
But in the end, they turned away
There was nothing left to do
The choice is yours, and yours alone
What path that you should take
But keep in mind, through all of time
Your soul has an eternal stake

Dark Welcoming Speech

I know who you are
I know where you've been
I know everything about you
To your tiniest sin
I am the one
Who bought on your pain
I am the one
Driving you insane
I am the reason
You're afraid of the dark
I brought on
That last remark
I revel in your torment
I laugh at your shame
I chuckle through your misfortunes
I clap when you're in pain
I can see it now
You're coming around
Soon you won't be able
To keep your soul aboveground
Listen to me
Hear what I tell
You are now damned
To my eternal hell
You had your chance
You turned the wrong way
Now you are here
And with me you shall stay

My Task

Waiting in the darkness
Pacing through the night
The future seems so certain now
Dreaming of the light
I know now what will happen
I've seen it in my sleep
I know what will happen
And that secret I must keep
I dream the dreams
Both day and night
Of wolves who dawn
Both black and white
In groups of three
They come to me
The meaning of which
Only now I see
The man in red
Who saved my life
The bracelet I found
To deliver from strife
The dragon
From the ground it came
Seven horns
Each with a name
These things together
Have revealed to me
A future that
I did not see
And so, Waiting in the darkness
Pacing through the night
The future seems so certain now
Dreaming of the light

A Fire

There's a fire in your eyes
Burning hotter than hell
There's an evil in your eyes
Like an angel who fell

The Mirror

When you look into the mirror
What do you see?
When I look into the mirror
I see everything but me
I see a way I did not look
I see a path I did not take
I see a tear I did not shed
I see a smile I did not fake
I see things
That no one should
I see things
You never could
I see the fire
I see the sea
I see it all
Inside of me
The struggle for balance
Between dark and light
The struggle for peace
An eternal fight
I see the future
I see the past
I see it all
As long as it lasts
I see the stars
Outshining the night
I see the planets

Internal light
I see the balance
I see the fight
I see the dark
I see the light
All of these things
Your mirror will reveal
When you look past you
To the you that is real
When you look into the mirror
What do you see?
When I look into the mirror
I see all that is me

# ABOUT THE AUTHOR

R.S. Gunn is a wife, a mother, a US Navy veteran, an ordained minister, and a published poet. She has traveled the world (only two out of seven seas) and holds multiple degrees, licenses, and certifications. She describes her personal style as comfy/classy. That just means when she has spent a few days in pajama pants, she throws on some lipstick because—classy. Above all else, R.S. Gunn is dedicated to her family. Her children serve as her inspiration both in writing and in day-to-day life. To learn more, visit her website at www.rs-gunn.com.

CPSIA information can be obtained
at www.ICGtesting.com
Printed in the USA
LVHW090901121119
637080LV00003BA/380/P